Her Roadside Rescues

Sea View House Book 4

LINDA BARRETT

Copyright (c) 2020 by Linda Barrett
ISBN-13: 978-1-945830-21-1

These stories are works of fiction. Names, characters, places, and incidents are either products of the author's imagination or used fictitiously. Any resemblance to actual events, locales, or persons, living or dead, is entirely coincidental.
All rights reserved.

No part of this publication can be reproduced or transmitted in any form without permission in writing from Linda Barrett

DEDICATION

To the Rescuers and the Rescued—may you have long healthy lives together and never be lonely again!

Cover art by Shelley Kay at Web Crafters

E-book and print formatting by Web Crafters

www.webcraftersdesign.com

CHAPTER ONE

Bartholomew Quinn pulled open the heavy door of the Diner on the Dunes, the regular hangout for his ROMEO buddies, and breathed in the aroma of good coffee.

"Hits the spot every morning, it does," he said, turning back to his longtime pals, Doc Rosen, Sam Parker, and Ralph Bigelow, along with Ralph's grown nephew. "Especially with another New England winter coming on." He pulled off the woolen hat he'd promised his family he'd wear, revealing his still-full white mane, and led his cronies toward the back of the eatery, where an empty table waited for them.

"They're predicting a bad one this year," said Ralph. "I'm glad you're still here to meet Brandon—my brother's son—before he moves into Sea View House." The man reached around and clapped his nephew on the shoulder.

"You mean before Bartholomew escapes to Florida!" grumbled Sam Parker, whose friendship with Bart spanned over fifty years. "But I'm glad for you, Bart. Warmer weather can't hurt."

"Thank you, thank you. I'm a happy man, and I can't disappoint my Honeybelle, now can I? She's not wintered here in years and doesn't want to! But I'll come back and forth. Like a-a snowflake, I believe they call it."

Applause met his ears, and his heart filled. Where else but in this town could a man derive so much satisfaction with his life? He raised his eyes to young Brandon Bigelow and extended his hand. "Welcome to Pilgrim Cove. I'm always happy to meet more family," he said. "That's what life's all about. And I'm particularly happy when Sea View House has tenants. You can take that fact to the bank!"

He turned at the arrival of more men. "Ahoy! Here's Joe Cavelli and Mike Lyons. Now we're almost a full house. Hope Lou didn't get lost in a book and Rick isn't out walking a beat."

He motioned them all to sit down at the table, in the center of which a sign proclaimed, *Reserved for ROMEOs.*

"Reserved for ROMEOs," read Brandon. "You guys must have a lot of clout around here."

"We sure do," replied his uncle. "Everyone knows we look out for the town." He glanced at Bart. "Tell him about it."

Bart Quinn made himself comfortable, fixed his gaze from one to another of the seven, and waved to Lou Goodman, who'd just joined them. "Come, come. We have bits and pieces to explain to this young man."

"The chief's just behind me," said the retired librarian, extending his hand to Brandon. "Hello, son."

Bart slapped his hand on the table and exclaimed. "With Rick O'Brien coming, we have a full house! The best kind."

##

Brandon Bigelow leaned back in his chair, sipped his coffee, and watched the show. Neither the Land of Oz nor Wonderland could outdo this Pilgrim Cove experience. Who knew that his quiet uncle was part of group led by a six-foot leprechaun who must have kissed the Blarney Stone more than a few times?

They called themselves ROMEOs—Retired Old Men Eating Out—the caretakers of Pilgrim Cove. In theory, every town could use a team like that, but Brandon preferred fewer theatrics. Fortunately, he was part of the audience, not one of the players.

Until he felt a pair of keen blue eyes focused on him. Until he felt seven curious pairs of eyes fixed on him. Until he fought the impulse to squirm under their spotlight.

"So, my boy," said Bart, "your uncle says you need a place to stay for a while."

"A short while," Brandon said with a sharp nod. "But no favors. I'll pay my way."

"That you will, boyo. But Sea View House is part of a trust and leased on a sliding scale. Rental is fair."

Nice. "My building is being turned into condos," said Brandon, "and I need new digs...hmm...fast. I've got two weeks to get out."

"Condo conversions happen," said Bart slowly. "I should know since I've been dabbling in real estate my entire life."

Ralph chuckled and joined the conversation. "Some dabbling! Bart is president of Quinn Real Estate and Property Management, which he runs with his granddaughter. You'll see it on Main Street. Big sign. Sturdy building with big windows in front. We keep it in tip-top shape. Just like we care for Sea View House."

A new side to his uncle. Almost verbose. Brandon shook his head, wondering what other surprises lay ahead.

"Thank you, Ralph," said Bart. "That's what I call a top-notch referral." His gaze pierced Brandon again. "I'm pretty sure you had more than two weeks' notice to vacate."

The man was probing. If he expected an in-depth explanation, he was going to be disappointed. "As a Realtor, Mr. Quinn, you can appreciate how scarce affordable apartments are in Boston."

Which was totally true but left out the major part of his story. The part that had kicked him upside down and backwards, that had distracted him to the point of losing track of everything in his life including his need for new living quarters. And now here he was, dependent on this man and a place called Sea View House.

"That I can, boyo, that I can."

Lost in thought, Brandon jerked himself to awareness again. Quinn was talking about the scarcity of places in Beantown.

"And now you find yourself in a pickle."

True enough. "And a pretty sour one at that," said Brandon.

The whole lot of them actually guffawed. Around the table, every single one. Brandon managed not to join them.

"Sea View House is a beauty," Bart finally said. "A big gray saltbox, with two apartments and a widow's walk on top."

"Right on the beach," said Sam Parker. "My daughter-in-law spent part of a winter in that house, too. The wind can blow hard, and take sand with it. But there's a cozy, safe feeling there, she always said. Was never afraid to be alone. And then, of course, Matt swooped in and scooped her up!"

"What a time that was!" the librarian chimed in. For the next two minutes, Brandon was regaled with more stories of true love matches at Sea View House than he wanted to know. Especially not after his recent relationship fiasco. Was it six months ago? Or longer…?

"This house sounds like a marriage factory," said Brandon, trying to be upbeat along with the men. "But while I'm interested in living on the beach, in such a unique place, I'm not interested in finding a wife. If that's the criteria for rental, then sorry, but I'm outta here. I'll take my chances at a motel." And blow a wad of cash.

Stunned silence all around. "But son," said Bart, "not a one who lived in that house ever was interested in romance! They were just like you. And then"—he gestured widely and spoke slowly— "the magic happened. Love happened. It's a powerful force, ya know. Why…it's as powerful as the ocean right outside the back door. It can happen to anyone, even to a young-at-heart old codger like me." His voice faded, and Brandon shook himself out of the spell the leprechaun so easily created.

"You have a way with words," said Brandon, "I'll grant you that. And if your stories make you happy…" He shrugged, leaving the thought unfinished. "But those people aren't me." He paused. "Perhaps you have a different property here that's available?"

In silent accord, the men eyed each other, but it was Quinn who spoke.

"Ach…no, no, Brandon. It's Sea View House, with the fair rental, or back to Boston with you. A sorry loss for all of us. Your uncle…" He shrugged and let his voice fade.

Ralph clapped Brandon on the back. "It will all work out. You'll see. So, Bart, is it the Crow's Nest or the Captain's Quarters for my nephew?"

Finally, they were getting somewhere.

"You've got the choice, boyo. The other tenant hasn't shown up yet. Don't quite know when." The old codger clasped his hands together over his stomach and leaned back. "You'll have better views upstairs in the Crow's Nest, where you'll see the mighty Atlantic in all her moods. But the apartment downstairs is larger, and there you can open the back door and plant your feet right into the sand. You can't go wrong with either."

Wonderland was starting to seem better. His uncle was great. His aunt, too. The entire ROMEO group was a hoot. Definitely a one-off. His imagination kicked in, and he felt a smile lurk inside. He could definitely come up with a creative business card to promote them, even if it was just for kicks. He had a feeling the man with the brogue would get the biggest kick of all.

"With a house on the beach, the choice is a win-win," said Brandon. "But I work from home and need some space, so I guess it's the Captain's Quarters for me."

"And what does Brandon Bigelow do to earn his way in the world?" asked a familiar voice.

Brandon studied each man around the table. Not one under sixty-five, he'd bet. He'd stick to basics. "I'm what's called a graphic designer. I use art and a computer to help businesses communicate with their customers." A few furrowed brows formed. He should be more basic. "I create things like business cards, book covers, and flyers." And a whole lot else or he wouldn't be self-employed.

The faces brightened. "Who's got one of our business cards with him?" asked Ralph.

"I never leave the house without a few in my wallet." Lou Goodman, the librarian, reached into his pocket, pulled out a folded piece of card stock, and gave it to Brandon. "If you ever need anything at all while you're in Pilgrim Cove, you've got friends."

Brandon stared at the oversized card. On one side, in bright red ink, was the word ROMEOs. The other side, in royal blue, listed every man's name, phone number, and special skill. His uncle was listed as Ralph Bigelow, Electrician.

The men all looked at him, faces eager, as if seeking approval. And in that moment, Brandon realized that "taking care of the town" was no joke to this group. They really cared. With that thought, and to his surprise, he felt the recent hard edge he'd acquired begin to soften.

"It's perfect," he said with a smile. "Couldn't have communicated better myself." He took out his own wallet and placed their card inside. "I'm keeping this one." He'd probably never need it, but it sure made the old guys happy.

"That's what they're for. We're just a phone call away."

"No texting, huh?"

"Don't be foolish, boyo," said Bart, holding up his hands. "With these big fingers, fuhgeddaboudit!"

Brandon was still chuckling as he and his uncle left the diner. Still chuckling until he heard Bart's voice again.

"Brandon Bigelow! I did mention another tenant at Sea View House, did I not? Any time now. But no worries. Separate entrances."

He'd forgotten about that, but it didn't matter. He'd lived his adult life in apartment complexes with neighbors all around. This would be no different.

##

Kathy Russo, surrounded by suitcases, grocery bags, and a laptop near her apartment door, reached out and hugged her grandmother. "I love you, Nonna, and I'll take very good care of Sheba while you're in Florida. She'll love the new place I'm renting." She kneeled down to rub the beloved golden retriever mixed breed and was rewarded with a happy whine.

"I know you will, Katarina," said the older woman, "but it's not only Sheba I'm concerned about. I worry about you, too."

"But—"

"I know. I know. You're a very capable young woman," interrupted Teresa, who started to pace. "I've heard you a hundred times. And I trust Bart Quinn with his offer of that house on the beach for you. He loves that town of his. Why he bothers going to Florida"—she shook her head— "I don't know."

Kathy laughed. "I think the answer is— hm...what's her name? Oh, Honey something. Honeybelle. Right? Your new condo neighbors sound great. I'm glad you met them."

"Good people, yes. And both from Massachusetts. But they won't be with you over the winter. You won't know anyone at all. I'm not sure this is a good plan." Teresa continued to pace. "You'll be hours away from the family."

Kathy sighed, remembering the tumult, chatter, football game hullaballoo, and general havoc wrung by her entire family on Thanksgiving Day. A mere twenty-four hours ago. Thirty years of family chaos was enough!

She led her grandmother to the nearby sofa. "Come sit a minute." She gently clasped the woman's hand.

"I'll be less than two hours from home, Nonna, and mostly because of traffic. You know I need a break. No one in this entire family respects boundaries. They call, they show up, they interrupt." She sighed deeply and shook her head. "Like last week—"

Nonna's eyes narrowed. "What happened?"

"I was on the phone with my boss at Mass Life, and Nicky came pounding on my door, calling my name. Elizabeth heard him and I had to apologize. It was so unprofessional! And, not to pat myself on the back, but my projects are important. She depends on me."

"Of course she does. You're a whiz with mathematics. Maybe you should have been a professor!"

That dream had passed, and she'd moved forward. "Just born with the math gene, I guess. Numbers are great. They don't talk back like some people..." Her family. She loved them for sure, but three brothers could easily drive her crazy. After her oldest brother got married last year, her younger one had adopted a protective brother role.

"If I don't get away," said Kathy, "I'll never get any writing done. I have absolutely no privacy here. And I like solitude. I'm not like the rest of them."

The woman stroked Kathy's hair and cheek. "They love you, sweetheart, but they don't understand you."

"They think they do. If I hear *absent-minded professor* one more time..."

Nonna laughed. "You're more like me. Our choices are different from theirs. We prefer to work alone and maintain an orderly life. Choosing a more solitary road is incomprehensible to them."

"Exactly right. I'm not an extrovert like the rest of the family. It's too exhausting!"

Nonna emitted a full-throated laugh. "I know exactly what you mean. I get worn out, too. We're the oddballs, my dear, but to be happy, you must stay true to yourself."

Her grandmother was one in a million, and Kathy adored her. In her quiet, steady manner, Nonna had defied tradition and her family, graduating from college and becoming a paralegal at one of Boston's most prestigious law firms. A perfect career for a woman who loved research and organizing information, and who couldn't care less about perfecting a recipe for chicken cacciatore. She remained true to herself even after she'd met her Roberto and fallen head over heels in love. He'd understood her. A perfect match for forty-five years.

She leaned into her grandmother and hugged her close. "Thanks, Nonna. I'm delighted not to be the only oddball in this family." The natural light faded from the room, and she glanced out the window. "It's clouding up. Want me to drive you home before I leave on my...ahem...journey to another galaxy?"

Teresa flashed a smile. "No, no. Not necessary. Pack the car and get started." She bent down to rub her pet. "Take care of my girl, Sheba. And she'll take care of you. Deal?" She held out her hand, and the rescue shook it with her paw. "Good girl." She glanced at Kathy. "Two good girls!"

With a rueful chuckle, Kathy said, "Ah, Nonna. I'm not sixteen anymore. But...if you'd like to think so..."

"What I'd like is for you to be safe, stay out of trouble, and"—she dug into her purse, finally producing her cell phone and shaking it— "call me!" She rose from the sofa and walked toward the door. "Be happy, Katarina." With one last kiss, her grandmother left and closed the door behind her.

Kathy stood quietly for a moment before turning toward the loving canine Teresa had rescued as a pup almost five years ago. Sheba sat at attention, her eyes following the young woman's every move.

"I'm not leaving you behind, girlfriend. Don't you worry. You and I are taking a road trip!"

The dog whined and trotted to the door, tail wagging.

Kathy looked at her in astonishment. "How the heck did you understand that?"

Sheba sighed, walked to Kathy's suitcase, and waited.

"Goodness, Sheb. Maybe we should have called you Einstein."

A small yelp came next.

Kathy laughed and started staging the rest of her belongings. "Okay, puppy," she said with affection. "Let's pack up the car and go to a place called Pilgrim Cove. You'll be able to run on the beach all you want. And I will be able to work in peace. No one to bother us." Exactly what she needed to keep up with two careers, especially her writing.

"Sea View House will be perfect."

LINDA BARRETT

CHAPTER TWO

Halfway to her destination, Kathy struggled to see through the onslaught of rain hammering on her windshield. The darkening sky in Boston had been the prelude to a true winter storm.

"Dang, Sheba. Those drops are turning into pellets of ice. Should have waited until tomorrow." She tapped the brakes, took a deep breath, and focused ahead. Sleet could turn the roads into slippery runways with little traction for her snow tires, good ones her dad had insisted she buy. She'd taken his advice—it was easier than arguing—and now was glad she had. But if the temperature continued to drop, the freezing rain would turn into solid ice.

"And we'll all be like bumper cars in an amusement park," she muttered, "slamming each other all over the place, snow tires or not."

The SUV in front of her had set a slow, steady pace, and Kathy adjusted her speed to match. *So far, so good.* In the rearview mirror, dim headlights shone through the sleet. *Just stay back.* Ten minutes passed, then twenty. The SUV continued to maintain the same speed even when the sleet changed again to rain.

"Rain's better than ice, Sheba, but I'm going to stay behind that SUV as long as it's going our way."

A whine came from the back seat as soon as the dog heard her name. Her grandmother's precious companion was tethered securely with a harness attached to the seat belt. Kathy could see the top of her blond head in the mirror.

A *rotary ahead* sign appeared. "I think we're getting closer, Sheb." Kathy reduced her slow speed further, easing the car into a gentle turn, and followed the circle around to the opposite side of the rotary before exiting. A straight path lay ahead, which, according to a dimly lit road sign, led to a bridge and Pilgrim Cove.

"I did my research, Sheb, and three miles after the bridge is all we have." She almost let herself relax. Almost. A native of New England winters, however, she knew better than to let her guard down when the prize was in sight.

"A quick visit to Bart Quinn for the keys, and we'll be cozy in our new place before we know it." Chatter, chatter. A real chatty Kathy. Not her normal habit. She grasped the wheel more tightly and spotted another road sign.

Welcome to Pilgrim Cove. Population: Winter—5000. Summer—Lots Higher.

"Well, someone has a sense of... Oh, oh...!" From the corner of her eye, she saw movement—maybe a dog or a cat—limping from the berm onto the road. The brake lights of the SUV blazed on. The car skidded and fishtailed left, right, and around, stopping only when it hit a tree on the right-side road edge, beyond the animal. Kathy tapped her brakes several times, kept control of the car, and pulled up in front of the damaged vehicle.

"Stay there, Sheba. I'll be right back." She opened her door and almost lost her breath in the cold air. The driver she'd happily followed for the last hour, confident that he or she knew what they were doing behind the wheel, had opened the driver-side door. Definitely a he with work boots and jeans. She ignored him, however, and raced to the injured animal. A whimpering, shaking black-and-white mix who favored his front right paw.

She squatted to the ground. "Oh, you poor thing." All the admonitions about not approaching strange dogs fled her mind, and she stretched out her arm toward the injured pup. "Come on, sweet boy."

A deep voice came from above and behind her. "No, I'm not hurt, but thanks for asking. My car's a mess."

"Just look at this poor pup," she replied. With not a glance at the man, Kathy focused on the dog and spoke softly. "Come on, sweetheart. You can trust me."

The mutt stood still and cocked his head. One ear came up. Kathy continued to coo and reach out. Slowly, the dog limped to her and she scooped him up. "You'll get warm in the car, fella. And that guy over there will have to get you to a vet."

The guy was on his cell phone. She walked over and parked herself next to him. No hat, dark hair blowing around. A frown marred his forehead. He definitely did not look happy.

"Cavelli's Garage, right?" He checked a paper he held. "Good. This is Brandon Bigelow, Ralph's nephew. We met at the diner. Yeah. I'm here now. But I seem to have had a run-in with a tree right outside town, near the neck."

He paused to listen, then studied his vehicle. "Yes, you'll need a tow truck. Thanks. I'll wait for you." He disconnected.

"No!" protested Kathy. "Call them back. You need to go to a vet. I'll give you a ride."

His wide-eyed expression said it all. He thought she was crazy. "Number one, this is not my dog and his care is not my problem. In fact, he caused me problems. Number two, I have to wait for the tow. And number three, why were you following me for an hour?"

"It's too cold to talk outside. I'll wait in my car until your tow comes, and then we'll go to the vet." Her heart pounded. Arguing with strangers was a lot harder than arguing with her brothers.

"You haven't been listening, sweetheart. This dog is not my resp—"

"Oh, yes he is," she interrupted. "You saved his life, and now he's yours—at least temporarily. You're responsible."

"And this is why I choose to work alone, live alone, and not get involved. It's better that way." With that, he turned and opened the door of his SUV.

"Well, sweetheart," she mimicked, "You're involved now. I'll be waiting to take you and poochie to the animal doctor. In the meantime, you can figure out where the vet's located." She leaned toward the rescue. "C'mon, buddy. Let's get you warm. Sheba will love hanging out with you for a while."

##

Brandon slid back into the driver's seat and took a deep breath. Hitting the tree counted as his third strike. First, the horrible breakup that caught him like a deer in the headlights, second, getting kicked out of his apartment building, and now, this…this stupid, unnecessary dog incident. And the woman! A small brunette with long wavy hair hanging down beneath her woolen hat. A petite brunette who thought she was an Amazon. If he weren't so annoyed, he'd laugh.

His palm itched, and his fingers started dancing. He chuckled at the familiar feeling and went with it. Reaching for a pad and pen, he quickly sketched the outraged Amazon with her hands on her hips, sporting an Avenger-type costume. He glanced toward her Honda Civic. Could see her bending over the rescue in the front seat. He turned back to his sketch and scattered a bunch of hearts around the figure. An Avenger with heart. Heck, nothing new there. Weren't they all like that beneath their costumes?

He pressed the voice option on his cell and asked for a veterinarian in Pilgrim Cove. He'd give Avenger woman the address and send her on her way. Hopefully, the collision shop could lend him a vehicle for a couple of days.

As he scribbled the information, he saw the woman leave her car and open the back door. A moment later, a different dog—a leashed one—jumped out and trotted toward the tree line to do some business. The woman was obviously a sucker for canines, exactly the right person to help the injured mutt.

He exited his vehicle with the vet's address just as the tow truck appeared. Action! Brandon felt himself relax, glad to get on with his day.

The driver parked and walked over. "Charlie Cavelli from the shop. My dad took your call." He extended his hand. "Lousy weather, but we'll tow her in and get her fixed up. You can ride with me."

"Great—"

"No, he can't. There's an injured dog involved, and we need to get him to a veterinarian."

Taking him off guard, she'd planted herself at his elbow.

Charlie looked from one to the other, his eyes narrowing as he gazed at the damaged vehicle. "Is that what happened here?" As he turned toward Brandon, a smile lurked. "Well, you did the right thing, and we'll get your CR-V fixed up ASAP. The dog might have come from old Rita Murray's collection. She lives way back over on the other side of the trees."

That was more information than Brandon needed or wanted to know. The man walked toward his truck, then turned. "Oh, you folks'll be needing Adam Fielding, left side of this main road as soon as you hit town. He's the vet around here. Excellent man. Our family trusts him."

Brandon dangled his research paper in front of Avenger woman. "Here you go. Good luck. I'll wait here while Charlie does his work."

Even in the waning light, Brandon could see renewed determination in her strong posture and set jaw. Her alert gaze pierced him. But it was her low-pitched voice that held him. "You saved his life," she began, "but he still needs help, and now you're going to walk away? I don't think so."

"Start thinking again."

She stood taller. "Then you consider this: if I go to the vet alone, I will have two dogs—one injured—in the car with me while I'm behind the wheel. Next thing you know, I might crash into a tree myself. Is that what you want?"

"Of course not!" The woman's imagination knew no bounds. It matched her ability to manipulate him.

"I knew it! I knew I could trust you." From a determined woman to a delighted girl.

Man, he had to straighten her out. "Nonsense. We're strangers. You don't know me at all. How could you make a judgment like that?"

A smile lit her eyes. "Stop sounding so tough. Why do you think I followed you on this horrible drive? You kept a steady, safe pace, eased to your stops, and signaled way in advance if you were changing lanes. I felt a lot safer than navigating through this crud all alone."

He recognized defeat when he met it. So strange that the Avenger trusted him without a personal meet, while it took a year for his ex-fiancée not to trust a future together. A corporate-world exec had caught her eye. And he had caught them—in bed.

"Okay, sunshine. You win this round." He turned toward Charlie, who was standing closer than he'd thought—and laughing.

"Buddy, you've got your hands full." He handed Brandon some paperwork.

Surprised at the man's assessment—and confused—Brandon could only ask, "What do you mean? We just met. Don't know each other at all."

This time a deep belly laugh lingered in the air as Charlie Cavelli took the signed papers and went to his truck. "But you will, my friend. You surely will."

A familiar feeling swept through Brandon, that down-the-rabbit-hole feeling he'd had in the Diner on the Dunes the week before. He shrugged it off. By tomorrow, he'd be back to his routines and the pleasure of being satisfyingly alone at Sea View House.

##

Kathy tossed her car keys to the man she'd followed. "You drive. I've got to hold little Rocky on my lap.

"How do you know his name?"

"I just gave it to him. Seems to me his life has been a rocky road, hm?"

The man shook his head. "He probably has a name. And a home…"

"Not a good home or he'd never have left. The only collar he has is a dirty piece of red string."

She opened the front passenger door. The dog lay exactly as she'd left him on the seat. Quiet. Resting. Breathing. Gently, she maneuvered her arms underneath him and maneuvered herself inside. Books and a carton took up all the floor space, so she folded her legs crosswise as best she could and wriggled onto the seat. Sheba whined and stuck her snout under Kathy's arm. "You're fine, girl. We're all just fine."

The man opened his door and Kathy felt Sheba stiffen. Barks emerged.

"A damn menagerie," he muttered, shoving something at her. "Here, can you take my laptop?"

"It's okay, Sheba," she said, putting his computer atop the book carton. "He's a nice guy, no matter how grumpy he sounds. His name is…sheesh…I don't even know it."

"No reason to. Consider our meeting a brief interlude." He tried to adjust himself behind the wheel. "You must be three feet tall. I'm a folded taco."

She giggled. "Sorry. I had to adjust the seat. My entire life is in this car, at least all the important stuff. So, no extra room." She stroked the dog on her lap over and over.

"I know the feeling well." He started the car, checked the mirrors, and pulled onto the road.

"Really?"

"Yeah, really."

"I don't like his loose coat, and I'm feeling some ribs underneath. Not a good sign."

He pointed ahead. "Tell it to the vet. Remember, he's about a mile up on the left. Keep your eyes peeled for the office. Cavelli back there told me this Adam Fielding is a sucker for strays. You're in luck."

She continued stroking the bedraggled mixed breed on her lap and heard the dog sigh. "I bet Charlie meant that the doc is tireless in finding good homes for his rescues."

"Spin it however you want, sunshine. We're almost there."

"My name is Kathy, and I'm not your sunshine or sweetheart. So, cut it out."

She heard his long whistle of acknowledgement. "Yes, ma'am. Kathy. Katherine. Kat."

"Katarina." She pivoted slightly in her seat. "Don't ruin your image. I'm really starting not to like you at all—even though you're a great driver."

His laughter filled the car. All the tension, the furrows, and tight mouth disappeared as her companion made a left turn into Dr. Fielding's driveway. "Maybe I'll come back as an Uber driver in my next life."

He parked the car and said, "Stay put until I ring the bell. It's still raining."

Like she cared. The entire day felt like an out-of-body experience. Since when did she make a habit of befriending strangers? Since when did she verbally spar with anyone? She lived a quiet life. By herself. On a computer. Calculating numbers, statistics, risk—as well as writing mysteries. And enjoyed writing so much that she'd left Boston and her family to find a quiet place. Right now, however, her road seemed as rocky as her rescued pup's.

A minute later, Uber-man was opening her door. "Let's go."

"You take Rocky," she said, offering him the dog. "I need to get Sheba."

He mumbled something, but scooped the dog up, while she untangled her legs and stood on firm ground.

A minute later inside the office, a smiling man and young girl greeted them and led them to an exam room in the back. "Let's get this boy on the table."

"Uh-oh, Dad. It's one of Rita Murray's."

"I've heard that name," said Kathy. She glanced at her partner-in- rescue. "Didn't Charlie mention that name when he came to tow the car?"

"No doubt," said the vet while running his hands over the dog. "It's a problem. Mrs. Murray thinks the red string is a collar, and that makes her the owner. Therefore, the dogs have a place to live." He sighed. "Doesn't work that way. This fellow is undernourished. Now, let's take a look at these feet."

"I'll be in the waiting room."

"But it's your dog…." Kathy protested.

Uber-man had suited action to words so quickly, however, she'd spoken to an empty corner. "Well don't let the door hit ya…"

"Squeamish?"

"I wouldn't know. Don't even know his name. It's been quite an adventure."

"That's life," said the vet in a satisfied voice. "Take your girl to the waiting room and leave her there. This rescue has fleas, a cut paw and malnutrition. Very normal for a homeless canine."

"Oh, my…" said Kathy, walking toward the door and motioning the Uberguy over. "Take Sheba for a few minutes." She leaned over to kiss her. "It's okay, girl. I'll be right back."

When she returned inside, Dr. Fielding's words offered some relief.

"I'll keep him overnight and doctor him, as my patients' parents like to say." He turned toward his daughter. "Sara, get some of the puppy chow and a bowl of water."

"I know, Dad. Puppy food is easier to digest, even though this one's not really a puppy anymore." She glanced at Kathy. "I love rescuing animals and finding homes. I'm glad you brought this dog here. And I'm so glad he really does have a new home."

"You'd better take those gorgeous dark eyes and dazzling smile into the waiting room and tell Uber man he's now a proud dog owner. He's the one who saved Rocky's life and hit a tree for his efforts."

The girl's eyes widened. "Wow! Then he's got to love him." She cooed at the dog. "Underneath all your dirt and matted fur is really a pretty boy." The youngster ran for the dog food, then darted into the waiting room, seeking her prey.

"She wants to be a vet, too, but she'll give away more than she earns," grumbled her dad while offering some chow to his patient.

"She'll be happy," said Kathy. "And she'll figure it all out." Like she had. Half corporate, half self-employed. And very happy.

The door opened and Uber man entered. "I left your daughter with Katarina's dog so I can wind things up here and be on my way." He reached for his wallet. "So how much will this little visit set me back?"

"Hold on," said Kathy. "What do you mean about winding things up? Rocky is yours. You can't just leave him and be on your way."

The man sighed. "He's really not, you know. I fulfilled my responsibility by bringing him here. I'm done."

Her heart broke a little. "Why did I ever think you were a great guy?"

He snapped to attention. "Poor judgment. You don't even know me."

Kathy straightened to her full five feet two inches and eyeballed him. "Right now, I don't even like you." Turning to the vet, she added, "Then Rocky is mine. Sheba was a rescue, too, and now look at her! She and I will take care of this newcomer."

CHAPTER THREE

Next time, he'd add lightning bolts to her costume.

In the silence that followed, Brandon could hear the ticking of the wall clock, the sound of Kathy's breath, and the slow chewing of the rescue as he ate his chow.

"Rocky boy needs a calm, stable home," said the vet. "You two are oil and water. So..." He addressed Kathy. "I know most folks around here. Are you visiting someone or just passing by?"

Her face lit up with that golden smile. "I'm definitely not passing by. Bart Quinn found the perfect place for me—a house on the beach—so I can work without interruption."

Quinn's name made Brandon's ears reverberate. The beach? No! Please no.

"I bet you mean Sea View House," said Fielding.

Her eyes glowed as if backlit by the moon, and his stomach tightened. *Of all the gin joints in all the world...*

"How did you know?" she asked.

"People in small towns know everything," continued the vet, "and everyone knows Bart Quinn. My wife stayed in that house a few years ago. That's where I met her. Well, I really met her in a bar, but..."

"And I could use a drink right now. A stiff one," said Brandon.

Startled, they both looked at him in confusion. His lips tightened. They'd both forgotten he was in the room. Well...two could play this little game.

"Quinn has a lot to answer for." He stared at Kathy. "Crow's Nest?"

Her head jerked back. Then she nodded slowly, her mouth pursed. He watched her dismay grow as she came to the right conclusion.

"Oh. My. God," she said. "You've rented the Captain's Quarters." In a moment, her unhappy surprise turned to laughter, which turned into giggles, and she actually held her stomach and tried to stop. "It serves you right," she said between gasps, "to think you could escape little Rocky."

He hadn't thought about Rocky in the last few minutes. Katarina the Avenger, however, would be hard to ignore.

"We need some rules," he said, trying to take the lead and avoid being pulled under by events.

"Tell you what, folks," said Fielding. "You can figure this all out later. Just make out a check or use a credit card to *Greys and Strays,* the small rescue center I founded behind the office. That's where Rocky will spend the night."

"How much?" asked Brandon.

"It's a donation. Up to you. Let's get Sara back here now so we can finish up."

Once at the reception desk, Brandon reached for his wallet. "I'll take care of this," he said to Kathy. "I imagine you'll be spending a fortune on other stuff for the hound."

"Whatever makes you happy."

"Finding another place to live would make me happy." After tossing his credit card to the vet, he pulled out the ROMEO business card. He'd call Quinn as soon as possible. All was not lost.

###

"I think we take a right on Outlook Drive," said Kathy, behind the wheel. "Which is coming up." She turned onto the street and gasped. "Look at that house! It's huge."

On the corner and outlined against the darkening sky, the two-story with third-floor attic loomed large.

"Sure looks it," said Brandon. "Pull into the driveway and take your dog for a walk. I want to make a call."

She gave him one of those exasperated-with-men looks. "If you're calling the garage about your things, don't bother. You can take my car and retrieve them. I don't mind."

He was hoping not to return to Sea View House, but he just nodded. "Thanks." He watched her lead Sheba to the curb and connected with Bart Quinn.

A total waste of time, as it turned out. "Nothing else is available?" asked Brandon in disbelief. "Yeah, I know it's winter at the beach. But…"

He listened to the fast-talking Realtor. "Nothing else is winterized? Mostly summer places?" The man talked more quickly than an auctioneer.

"Yeah, I met her. If you want more details, call your pal Joe Cavelli. His son will have filled him in by now."

He listened to a fast discourse on where the keys were, disconnected, and threw his head back to look at the sky. The clouds were breaking up. Stars were beginning to show themselves, some twinkling brightly, others dim. It was a big world out there. A universe. He cocked his head and listened. From the near distance, he heard a rhythmic whoosh—the sound of waves hitting the shore right behind the house. Where else could he find such a place?

He'd been looking forward to this getaway. Grateful for it. Grateful to his uncle for suggesting it. Quinn was a character, a big personality. The man knew what he wanted and pounced while, at the same time, attracting a stable of loyal friends to help him get things done. A man's man. And, he guessed, a woman's man, too.

He refocused on his immediate surroundings. On Kathy Russo, who, with her dog, seemed to be waiting for him to say something.

Walking toward her, he extended his hand.

"I'm Brandon Bigelow, a self-employed graphic artist, nephew of a ROMEO, recently of Boston, now of Sea View House. If we're going to make this work, we need some rules."

Her hand got lost in his, reminding him that superheroes always projected larger than life. Chuckling silently, he turned so she wouldn't see his smile.

"Let's decide those rules tomorrow. We've got other things to do first." She waved toward the car. "If this isn't unloaded, then you can't fill it with your stuff."

"I can lease a car for—"

"Don't be an idiot. It's getting late, and taking mine is more practical. But we have to figure out how we get into the house."

He pointed toward the left. "Side entrance. Key's under the mat. We're not in Boston anymore, Dorothy."

"And I am so glad!"

##

She released the trunk lock, and he started lifting suitcases, duffel bags, and cartons of books. "Are you taking a reading vacation?"

"I'm a working woman. Those are mostly reference books plus some fiction. I've got many more books on my e-reader."

The keys were exactly where Bart Quinn said they'd be. Kathy found the light switch and let Sheba run upstairs.

"She's a lot faster than we are," she joked, as she followed with a duffel bag and her computer.

The staircase led to a landing with another door, where Sheba sat, waiting.

"Okay, girl. Let's see." Kathy turned the same key into the lock and swung the apartment door open. She found the wall switch and light flooded the space.

"O-oh…a country kitchen! Huge. Perfect!" She ran toward the oversized table and put her computer down before reaching into the duffel bag to retrieve Sheba's bowls. She filled one with water, then turned to see Brandon coming from the hallway.

"Didn't know which bedroom you wanted…" he began.

She jogged past him, past two closed doors, and then saw one large and one small bedroom facing each other. The larger room had an oversized desk and chair.

"I'll work my day job in here." She called out to Brandon, "Did you come across a second computer?"

"This one?"

She snatched it and put it on the desk. "Okay, now I'm set. Two work spaces. I'm happy. Let's finish up."

Twenty minutes and several trips upstairs later, not a square inch of kitchen counter space was visible. Bags of groceries covered the area.

Brandon grunted at it. "Did you think you'd be at the North Pole? You look ready to weather a siege."

"That is not my doing!" Annoyance filled her. "My mother thinks I'll starve." She reached into a bag. "Oh, for crying out loud, she cooked, froze, and packed it."

"Sounds like a good mom."

"Depends on your definition." She lifted plastic storage bowls of meatballs, sauce, chicken. "I know how she thinks. In this weather, food would not spoil." She put it in the fridge. "And it didn't. It's safe to eat. My dad must have been in on it. He's got a second set of keys to my place. Dang! Mom's tentacles...she wanted them to reach to Pilgrim Cove." She twirled in place and pointed at Brandon.

"Do not be born into a big, noisy, nosy, opinionated, and overbearing family if you want to keep your sanity! Got it?"

"The thought gives me a rash." His serious voice was belied by eyes that gleamed.

"And stop laughing."

"Truth is that I haven't laughed as much in one day in a very long time."

Silence prevailed—for a moment. "I hope you'll be able to laugh at the bill for your poor car." She tossed him the keys to her Honda. "Good luck. I'll help you when you get back."

"Not necessary. I travel light...er than you."

"Anyone would," she admitted with a sigh.

He shrugged. "But we still need to talk about—"

"The rules of sharing Sea View House."

He nodded sharply. "No offense. But I'm not here to socialize."

"That makes two of us. And I wasn't planning on having a downstairs neighbor, either." She eyed him straight on. "Let's keep our distance and maybe this won't be so awful after all."

##

The news about his car wasn't good. Body work, alignment check.

He thanked Charlie for the quick estimate of cost and pickup date, unloaded his stuff into Kathy's car, and asked the man for directions to a grocery store. He certainly didn't have the food supply Kathy had.

He paused in the soup aisle and loaded up on a variety. Hot dogs, rolls, frozen pizza, milk, yogurt, coffee, bread…some bananas, apples. He went to the deli section and bought a cooked chicken. Paper products next. By the time he got to the checkout line, his cart was almost full. He'd be good for two weeks. Hopefully.

He pulled into the Sea View House driveway, automatically checking the upstairs windows. Dark. Maybe she'd shut the hall light and gone to bed. He'd have to return the keys the next day. The temperature had dropped again, and he made quick work of bringing his groceries inside.

As he took off his parka, a knock on the back door was followed by a "Hey there," and suddenly the kitchen seemed crowded with people, grocery bags, and dog.

"Woof." Sheba trotted over and looked at him with her big brown eyes, waiting expectantly.

"Pet her. She likes you."

Brandon glared at the dog's owner. "I have no idea why." But he knelt down to accommodate the request. "Good girl, Sheba. Good girl."

"Sheba gives love and expects love," said Kathy. "She trusts people now. My grandmother saved her..."

His ears perked up as he unloaded the food. The woman thought she was softening him up about the rescue they'd brought to the vet.

"Quit while you're ahead. I'm not taking Rocky."

"If you did, you'd have the most devoted friend for years to come. Much better than people."

"Now *that* I can believe." As he watched in amazement, she began loading the dairy into the fridge. "So let me understand this. Sheba belongs to your grandmother, but you, yourself, don't seem to live with man's best friend."

"If you had as many brothers, cousins, aunts, and uncles dropping in and out of your place, you wouldn't add to the chaos, either." Suddenly, she seemed unsure of herself. Maybe tired. She didn't meet his gaze. But, to his amazement, in the next moment, she turned on him.

"Why are you eating all this canned soup? Don't you know how much sodium is in each one?"

He pushed the soup away and returned the car keys. "We're done here. Good night. Go home."

She took the keys, spoke to the dog, and headed outside without another word to him.

The silence echoed. So maybe he'd bullied her a little. But finally, peace and quiet prevailed, just the way he wanted. In fact, if he could believe what she'd said earlier about keeping distance between them, she wanted a quiet life, too. Never friends but perfect housemates.

CHAPTER FOUR

"That short walk to the curb didn't count, Sheba. I promised you a run on the beach, and that's where we're going now." After a quick breakfast of toast and coffee the next morning, Kathy clipped on Sheba's leash, put on her own navy parka again, and clambered down the stairs to the outside door.

Crisp air, clear skies, and a temperature in the thirties greeted her. Kathy inhaled the clean, briny smell of early winter next to the ocean, just as delicious as she'd imagined it would be. Leading Sheba to the right and passing the backyard of the house, she crossed a row of dunes and found herself on the beach. The sand was packed down after the recent freezing rain. A harder surface than when sunbaked, but perfect for running.

"Ready, Sheba?" She extended the leash and started to jog alongside the dog. Soon the strains of moving day disappeared, and she savored her surroundings. She waved to another hardy soul, a woman in a woolen cap, who ran with two young boys. The three waved back at her.

"Sea View House?" the woman called.

"Yes."

A victory salute and a chorus of "Yay" from all three as they passed by.

"Weird but friendly, huh, Sheba? But it doesn't matter since I'm not actually going to make real friends with anyone here. We're only temporary residents."

She started to head back to the house, but Sheba pulled on her leash. "No chasing seagulls, sweetheart. I'm not sure you'd return to me when I called you back. I'll have to ask Nonna."

"Woof." She pulled again.

Coming at them from behind was a familiar figure, also dressed for a run.

"Oh, that's why you spoke," she said to the dog.

Brandon nodded as he passed them and continued on.

"Well, okay, then. Message received."

Once back at her door fifteen minutes later, she paused to catch her breath. "Do you even have the energy to climb upstairs, Sheba?"

The golden retriever mix wasted no time in scampering up, then looked down at Kathy, who followed at a slower pace. "Okay, girl. You win. And what's this?"

Taped to her door was a handwritten note in all caps.

VET CALLED.
YOUR DOG IS READY FOR PICKUP. TODAY.

"For goodness' sakes, Sheb. I bet Dr. Fielding never used those words. Pickup. Like an order of fast food!"

She knew she was venting, so disappointed in her housemate for not stepping up. And now, she'd have to provide poor Rocky with a home, at least for a while. Maybe Dr. Fielding would find folks who'd want to adopt him. The veterinarian did run a rescue center, after all.

She entered her apartment, searched online for his number, and got advice about what to buy for Rocky. Looking longingly at her personal computer and array of folders at one end of the kitchen table, she sighed with remorse. Evenings and weekends were reserved for her writing. She'd earned some praise—and royalties—for her first self-published mystery and was now halfway through the second in the series. Success with readers required a steady rate of book releases. And that required her butt to be in the chair!

Her fingers itched to be on the keyboard. She knew exactly where she'd left off in the story. "Just one peek, Sheba."

In five minutes, she was in deep, and two hours later, she stood and stretched in every direction. The apartment came into focus again. Sheba, who'd been napping at her feet, stood quietly, watching her every move.

Kathy glanced at the clock. "Holy Toledo, Ohio! Time's flying. And now we've got some shopping to do." She rubbed her companion on the scruff. "But it was a great session. Keep your paws crossed for me. And let's hope Rocky is a good boy."

She ate a quick lunch, leashed Sheba, and ran down the stairs. They'd head for the pet and supply store just outside of town that Dr. Fielding had suggested. Rocky had weighed in at fifty-two pounds but, according to the vet, needed to gain more muscle mass in a loving home with regular meals.

"He's a mix of poodle and black lab," Dr. Fielding had said, "maybe with something else, and he could hit sixty pounds with the right care. That would do it."

"Sixty pounds? Oh, my..."

"That shouldn't be surprising to you. I'd guess your Sheba weighs in at about fifty-five."

"Really? She-she seems more delicate than that. Delightful to have around and graceful running on the beach."

Fielding's laugh echoed in her ear. "Nice description. Her flowing hair can mislead you. Well, Rocky's a good boy, too, Ms. Russo. Just needs a good home—a lot of love and knowing who's boss."

She gulped. "Are you talking about me?"

"Is Bigelow out of the picture?"

"For sure. And not for lack of trying on my part. And let me be honest, I'll keep him for now. But just until you find a permanent home. I've got Sheba, too..."

"I see," he said slowly. "But it's still better for Rocky if he goes with you. Sheba is a happy girl. You know what you're doing. The only difference is that now you'll be the alpha of a little pack.

"A little pack?"

"Not to worry. We'll talk more when you get here."

Kathy hung up slowly. The alpha? All she'd wanted was a quiet, calm life at the beach. Just her and Nonna's perfect rescue. She had no experience in training a dog. Or in handling an injured one. She had no desire to be the "alpha."

"Well, Sheb," she said, standing tall and squaring her shoulders. "Looks like we're adding to the family. At least for now. I'm counting on you to help out with your new younger brother. Someone has to give the poor baby a home. It won't be Brandon, the Uber man, and it can't be—what's her name? Old Rita Murray."

##

"Wow! He cleaned up well."

Kathy could barely recognize the wavy-coated black dog who waited for her in the vet's office. She stood next to the exam table where Rocky lay quite contentedly after greeting her with a slow-wagging tail. Not as excited as Sheba would be when Kathy walked into a room, but with a cautious recognition.

"In addition to his malnourishment," said Dr. Fielding, "he's suffered an abrasion on his front right paw on the pad. Sharp ice, stones, or pebbles could have done that. He's spent a lot of time outside, not only yesterday but before then, too."

She bent over Rocky's leg to see the wound better. "So, he scraped his pad and it hurts."

"Exactly. That's why he was favoring it. Fortunately, there were no deep cuts. An abrasion, however, can get infected like any wound can. So, we're disinfecting it with betadine and then putting antibiotic ointment on it." He suited action to words, speaking quietly to the dog as he worked. "Finally, we're cushioning the pad, then wrapping the foot in gauze, and putting a plastic bag over the whole shebang." He used paper tape to hold the plastic in place.

Kathy's stomach tightened. "That's a lot of responsibility," she gulped. "What if…"

"I'm only a phone call away and live pretty close, too."

"Right." She pasted on a smile and looked at Sheba. "We can do this, partner. Can't we?"

Sheba stood on her hind legs, leaned against Kathy, and woofed. Rocky looked at her from the tabletop and emitted a short bark.

"Ready to go, fella?" asked the vet, who lifted him and gave him a hug before placing him on the floor.

"You've been a good boy, and you're going to be just fine in your new home." He looked at Kathy. "Rocky's housebroken, so you'll know when to take him out. Remember to use plastic bags to keep his paw dry outside. Just for a few days."

She nodded, smiled, and attached Rocky's leash while butterflies danced a tarantella in her belly. Rocky's care sounded like a full-time job.

With tail wagging, Rocky headed for Sheba but started to limp immediately. Kathy instinctively crouched down and rubbed his neck. "Aw, baby. You'll feel better soon. We'll go slowly." She received a lick for her efforts and stood up again.

"I'll walk you out," said the vet. "I've got a bag of special chow for him. No table food, not even Sheba's food. But make water freely available. For both of them."

"I need a rule book," she laughed. "Maybe I'll go to the library...uh, there is a library, isn't there?"

"Of course, but in the meantime, take this basic dog care book. That's all you'll really need. And by the way—thank you for doing a very good deed. I'll be visiting Rita Murray's place very soon and shutting her down...again. Other rescues will fill my center immediately."

A pack of bedraggled dogs filled her vision. Filthy and skinny, limping like Rocky did. She looked down at her beautiful rescue, ready to start his new life. Ready to trust her. A corner of her heart tore. "Okay, boy. We'll figure it out. You'll live with me."

##

With Sheba in the back seat and Rocky in front with her, Kathy slowly drove back to Sea View House. The vet had a point about the plastic covering. The ground was still wet in many places from the rain and ice. The lawn had to be soaked, too. She planned to pull into the driveway and park as close to her side door as possible.

She turned right from Main Street onto Outlook Drive and headed for the house just a bit ahead—where a big, black old-model Lincoln Town Car sat in her driveway, thwarting her practical plan. Dang it. She needed that close spot. Did her neighbor have company? She dismissed the thought. Brandon's uncle was still in Boston, visiting Brandon's parents for the rest of the Thanksgiving weekend. Brandon knew no one else— except Charlie from the car place.

It had to be a rental car. But a big Lincoln? Just didn't fit him. Hmm...it might have been the only thing available in this small town. But the man didn't have to rent a car at all! A mix of anger and disappointment washed over her. While she wanted her privacy, she'd never in her life made enemies while seeking it. Until now. This guy obviously wanted nothing to do with her. Total separation. She took a deep breath. Okay. She could live with that, but she'd prefer some respect along with it.

She sat up taller and looked from one of her charges to the other. "Okay, pups. How shall we do this?" Rocky *couldn't* run, and Sheba *wouldn't* run. She'd take them both and get Rocky's supplies afterwards. A minute later, with both leashes in her hand, she began to walk the dogs up the driveway.

Rocky set a slow pace, and Sheba adjusted her usual happy stride to match that of her new friend. A frisson of worry melted from Kathy. She was capable of caring for them both. Her Pilgrim Cove adventure would work out—despite Brandon's attitude.

Men's rumbling voices reached her when she arrived at her door. The leashes tautened as the dogs reacted, too. Brandon and a tall man with a leonine head of white hair appeared from around the back, from Brandon's kitchen door.

"Ahoy, lassie! You must be Teresa's granddaughter!"

"I am, indeed," Kathy replied. "And you must be Bart Quinn, the man I must thank for the rental of this wonderful place." Despite the neighbor.

The Realtor beamed. "Wonderful it is, lass. And magical, too." He walked closer, instantly surrounded by dogs wanting his attention, but he focused on Kathy.

"Is that right, Mr. Quinn? I can offer you a lot of adjectives to describe the house and the beach...but magical? I don't think so. It's a beautiful clapboard and cement house."

He gestured widely behind him. "Come over, lad," he said while still speaking to her. "Was I not just telling this good man how very special Sea View House is?"

Kathy darted at glance at her neighbor, who rolled his eyes.

"Oh, our Mr. Quinn did a lot of talking, he did," replied Brandon with a nod to the Irish brogue. He leaned down to pat Rocky, who was trying to jump on him.

"We're just a fingertip in the ocean," Quinn continued, "this peninsula we live on, with the mighty Atlantic on one side and Pilgrim Bay on the other. I know every street, house, and every person who calls this place home. So when I say magic happens here, I know what I'm talking about!"

Kathy could see in his bearing, hear in his voice that the man certainly believed his own words.

"So, Mr. Quinn," she said calmly, "could you give us a rational example of this magic you're referring to? Just...you know...make sure we understand?"

But Quinn just laughed. "A 'rational' example? There speaks the mathematician! There are plenty of miracles that happened here, but you're going to find that out yourselves. In fact, there's a journal inside. If you read it, you'll understand plenty."

He started walking toward his Town Car but paused and looked back. "I know about Rita Murray and her troubles. Glad to see you helped out. The good Dr. Fielding might need you again. That's what we do in this town. I'll tell your grandma when I see her this week." He pointed at Kathy's car. "Got keys?"

"I'll do it," said Brandon, glancing at the leashes.

While they waited, Bart handed her a large ROMEO business card, "Just in case." Glancing at it, she recognized the Bigelow name. Brandon's uncle.

"You sure do have connections, Mr. Quinn. My grandmother and Brandon's uncle. Is that how you get your tenants?"

"Lassie, lassie. The tales of Sea View House would take hours to recount. Read the journal."

"If I ever find the time…"

She remained in the driveway until the jockeying was over and Bart waved to them from behind the wheel.

Brandon returned her keys, a signal, it seemed, for Rocky to step closer to him. "You've got a home now, Rock. You're one lucky dog."

Kathy bit her tongue. True, Brandon could have stepped up and adopted him, but not everyone was a dog lover. At least the man had avoided killing Rocky at a cost to his wallet.

"Come on, pups. It's getting dark and colder. Time to go home. Maybe your new mom will get some writing done tonight." She led her charges to the door, opened it, and looked at the long flight up. Then looked at Rocky. No way could he navigate without further damaging his paw.

She dropped Sheba's leash. "Go on up, baby. I'll bring your new friend."

Sheba didn't move. "All right. We'll try something else." She squatted, scooped Rocky into her arms, took one step, and started to lose her balance. "Ahh!" Falling backwards, she was caught by a pair of strong arms.

"Easy, Kat. Easy. Give him to me, and I'll take him up."

Nothing on this trip had been easy. Resting against Brandon was tempting—very tempting—but she didn't want the occasional favor from him. She wanted more. A lot more.

She twirled, placed the dog in his arms, and took a deep breath. "He'll have to be carried up and down many times over many days, which is ridiculous. So here's the deal: either you take him to live with you downstairs, or we change apartments."

CHAPTER FIVE

Like a glowing ember, she was back in character. An Avenger. Her eyes implored, her chin rose high, and her posture brooked no argument. For her chutzpah, he'd give her half a win.

"I'll keep him with me—for now—and only for your sake. I won't be responsible for you falling down the steps and breaking your pretty neck while carrying him."

"Well, I suppose that's something." She turned her head, but he saw a tiny smile at the corner of her mouth.

"That's everything, kiddo. Count on it. As soon as the paw heals, he's yours. Enjoy the rest of your evening." He stepped outside.

"Not so fast, *kiddo*. His chow and meds are in the car. I'll bring them to you and give you some instructions."

He let her door slam behind him and carried the dog around the back, into his kitchen, where his computer and a stack of folders lay on the table. A designated workstation.

"Well, Rocky. I can't carry you around all day, so let's see what's happening." He placed the dog on the floor, where he stood still while keeping his eye on Brandon. "I'm not going anywhere, Rock." Brandon stepped back and motioned the dog to him. "Let's see you walk."

The dog limped over, and Brandon scooped him up again. "Okay, my man. Let's rest it." He stepped through to the living room, grabbed a cushion from the sofa, and put it on the kitchen chair next to his own.

"Let's first acknowledge, Rock, that your life is going to be pretty boring for a few days until you can run around again. Hopefully you'll sleep a lot, which would be best for both of us."

He heard the sound of his door opening and closing. "Here are the supplies." Kathy deposited them on the table.

"Twenty pounds of chow," he said, "should last until he's with you again. That's for sure."

She shrugged. "He's supposed to have small feeds several times a day. Here's the ointment, gauze, and sterile pads for his paw. And...a bunch of poop bags. I'll set up a trash container in the back." She walked to Rocky and removed the plastic wrap. "Only use plastic when he goes outside. It's for protection from the elements. The wound should air out inside."

She started to leave and turned back. "Here's the basic dog care book Dr. Fielding gave me, and oh, for Pete's sake! Take off his leash while he's inside. Even I know that."

"Has anyone ever mentioned how bossy you are?"

"Never."

He was pretty good at reading people, and she hadn't struck him as a liar before. But still he probed. "Oh, come on. Really? You've been nonstop bossy today."

He watched her nose crinkle, brows furrow. She actually gave it some thought.

"Not unless you mean my brothers. But they are truly overbearing and never listen to me anyway, so that doesn't count."

Shaking his head, he muttered, "I'd love to ask their opinion."

And there it was. Her smile. The enchanting smile that could light up the night.

"I bet you'd just love to chat with my brothers, but you're not going to have the chance. No family allowed for at least three months, or maybe until Nonna returns from Florida. Just Sheba and me. Alone. Which all sounded wonderful until—well, you know." She gave Rocky a hug. "I really have to earn a living while I'm here."

"So do I." He waved toward the dining room. "I'll be setting up in there, too. I need the space of the Captain's Quarters. Which is why," he admitted ruefully, "I took Rocky in. Your place is much smaller."

She dimpled up again. "Then I'm doubly glad you got the downstairs. You know, despite our unusual beginning, this...this sojourn of ours might work out for both of us."

Her words made him pause. Sojourn. A stop-over. A temporary residence. A respite. "I'll drink to that."

"I didn't notice any wine when you unpacked," she said with a laugh. "But I'll raise my empty glass, too."

Nice gesture. But he had to chuckle.

"What?" she asked. "What did I say?"

He took Rocky's bowl, filled it with water, and placed the dog on the floor next to it. "I'm simply wondering how long our peaceful interlude will last."

"That's up to you, Brandon. Work on it." She escaped through the door and, admittedly, had the last word.

But not the last laugh. That woman could make him laugh.

##

A peaceful Sunday. The day progressed as Kathy hoped all her subsequent days in Pilgrim Cove would. First, a run on the beach with Sheba, followed by an easy breakfast, and then a day of research and continuing her novel. Her actuarial projects for the insurance company would take over most of the next day and throughout the week. Most people might think it unusual to be have both a math side and an artsy side, but she disagreed. Solving a mystery—her favorite genre—was the same as solving a puzzle. Designing a mystery was doing it backwards. It was fun. Challenging. She loved it.

She browsed through her printed manuscript, rereading the last chapter she'd written to set her mind on the story. Then she focused on the electronic version. Just two or three more chapters for the protagonist, Dana Moretti, to bring this case to a close. Dana had been a delight and a challenge to develop, and with each scene, Kathy got to know more and more about her personal life and background. And her personality. A mystery wouldn't pack the punch she wanted without the reader caring about the main character. And being curious, too.

"If we were home, Sheba, we'd be in the middle of a huge Sunday dinner with the parental units right now, and with a dozen voices vibrating off the walls."

Sheba stared at her with concentration and then whined.

"Don't you think this quiet life is much better?"

As if on cue, her cell phone rang. And there they all were—her family—on the extension phones, wanting to know all about her trip. Had she met Bart Quinn? How was the beach? How was Sheba?

As she tried to explain, a knock sounded at the door. Brandon stood there, holding Rocky. She motioned him in. "Is anything wrong with Rocky?" she whispered before speaking into the phone. "I've got company, folks. Talk to you later." Next week would work.

"And just when I was celebrating the quiet..." she joked to Brandon, "the entire Russo clan popped in." She mock-slapped her temple. "So how's it going?" She scratched the dog's head. "How are you, Rocky?"

"Rocky's just fine," replied Brandon. "Actually, it's been a good day for me, too. Is your offer of the car still open? I need it for a few minutes." He put the dog on the floor.

"Sure. Take your time." She tossed the keys to him, and he disappeared.

"Well, Rock, he was in a hurry, but it's good to see you, too." Sheba must have agreed, because she came right over to inspect her new friend, who definitely wanted to play.

Interesting how Sheba schooled him, nudging him to stay down as if she knew he had to take it easy. She stretched out next to him, whether for comfort or company, Kathy couldn't tell. "You're one smart doggie, Sheba. Smarter than a lot of humans." The dog's tail wagged hard in acknowledgement. Kathy smiled, shook her head, and jumped back into her manuscript

##

Brandon stood inside Kathy's door, watching her work. Sometimes, her fingers flew over the keyboard but usually paused right afterward, slowing to a measured *tap, tap, tap.* Then she'd raise her head to examine the screen and mumble to herself. A frown line, a smile. A nod. He enjoyed watching the process. Finally, however, he cleared his throat. She jumped, her hand going over the heart.

"Oh, my God, Brandon. You scared me witless. You're so quiet."

"Sorry about that. But witless?" He shook his head. "That doesn't describe you."

She blushed a dusky rose color, her hand moving from her heart to her neck. He'd been sincere and certainly hadn't meant his words to be flirtatious. In fact, a personal relationship was exactly the opposite of why he was visiting. He wanted to set up some rules.

"I bought a couple of bottles of wine," he said, taking them out of the bag. "To make real that empty toast we had."

"O…kay," she replied with a question in her voice.

"I have a proposition for you about these living arrangements that I think will work well."

She pointed downstairs. "You're there and I'm here. Works well for me."

"'And never the twain shall meet,'" he quoted. "I'm self-employed, Kathy. I speak with clients all day long and work on their projects. Any spare time I have is going to this dog you saddled me with. And to finding another apartment in Beantown."

Her eyes narrowed. "And you think I want to waste your time—with what? Romantic detours? You think I want to distract you from your career?" She waved at her table. "Does it look like I'm idle?"

"No!" he replied. "And that's the point. We're both here to accomplish the same goals. But you can be very distracting, and I can't afford that. So, let's make a deal: a three-month, hands-off, working arrangement. No socializing at all except for emergencies."

He thought she wouldn't reply. Instead, she stood, took the bottle of red, and produced a corkscrew from a kitchen drawer. She eyed him as she decanted and handed him a glass when she'd finished.

"Sounds to me like my housemate had a bad breakup. And not too, too long ago." She raised her glass. "So here's to new beginnings for you, and to zero distractions in a magical house."

He almost choked on his wine. How could she have figured out about his breakup with Amber? He'd said nothing. Absolutely nothing. And his uncle hadn't even met Kathy yet and couldn't have mentioned it.

"Seems you're looking for a new beginning as well," he said. "So right back at you." He took a sip. "But don't tell me you buy into Quinn's nonsense."

She looked startled for a moment, then raised her chin. "I'm trying to keep an open mind."

"Who are you kidding?" he asked. "You sound like you're reciting a line in a play. Magical. Fantasyland—and you, a mathematician."

Her sharp glance followed by another blush had guilt written all over her. "I am such a bad liar. It is a bunch of nonsense. I'm surprised, though, that you picked up on how I earn my living."

"Bart mentioned it, and I remembered." He pointed to his head. "Almost a photographic memory. It's not necessary but comes in handy for a graphic artist."

"Hmm. I bet it has its pluses and minuses."

Smart woman. Definitely a minus. His unexpected discovery of Amber with her lover boy was seared into his brain. Every detail of the bedroom—the pillow, strewn clothes, his leg over hers... He'd always believed in a picture being worth a thousand words—that's what his career was based on. But he never thought he'd be a victim of its awful truth.

"Brandon? Brandon? Where are you?"

Her voice brought him back to the moment, and he jumped in. "So if we're good with this arrangement, I'll just take Rocky and go."

"Not yet."

"What?"

She opened her fridge and took out a large bowl. "The wine is wasted without a meal. Despite my complaints the other day, my mom is a great cook. You won't get better Italian anywhere."

Tempting, but the woman hadn't listened at all. No distractions!

She busied herself at the counter. "I know what you're thinking. But we can start that in the morning. Everything seems better after a good meal. Just ask any of my brothers!"

He began to laugh. Perfect. No chance of entanglement with a pretty lady sporting a sunshine smile who viewed him as a brother.

##

Although the weather didn't improve during the next week, Kathy looked forward to her beach runs with Sheba and kept the two-a-day habit. It was often full dark by the time she returned to the house in the late afternoon. By Friday, the vision she had for her stay in the town was being realized. Two jobs, no interruptions. Excellent progress in both areas. And a paycheck from Mass Life deposited directly into her account.

As she'd explained to her mom a day earlier, "Time is flying. I'm working hard and never lonely. Sheba is the greatest gift! And when I'm writing, I've got lots of people to keep me company."

Of course, her mother thought she was nuts. "You made them up, Kathy," she insisted. "They're make-believe!" But Kathy knew her story characters so well, she chatted to them as though they were real people and shared their frustrations as they struggled—even though she controlled the plot! It was so hard to explain. And harder for others to understand. As long as readers enjoyed her mysteries, however, she figured she was doing something right. And so did Marsha, the freelance editor she'd hired. The writing was definitely a job for one person, but shaping the story to be as perfect as possible needed the expertise of other professionals.

Now she slipped on her parka, opened the outside door, and attached Sheba's leash for their second outing. "Ready, girl?" The dog danced around her. Born ready for an adventure, Sheba never refused an invitation to go out. They clambered down the flight to the entryway.

"We haven't seen Brandon and Rocky in a while," said Kathy, cracking the door open. "We must keep missing each other... I don't even have his phone number."

"We should rectify that."

Kathy startled at his voice. Her downstairs neighbor stood on the other side of the door. A scruffy-faced Brandon in a fleece-lined hoodie, holding Rocky's leash while the dog pranced around him and toward Sheba.

"You scared me." He looked darn good. Casually sexy and comfortable with it. Scruffy beards worked on all men, Kathy told herself. But those green eyes, glinting with humor—that's what he could claim as his own.

"Will you please teach him some manners, Sheba?" Brandon said, leaning against the doorframe. "He never stops playing." His chuckle belied the complaint.

"You're in a good mood today," said Kathy. "In fact, an excellent one. You must have had as great a week as I had."

"Two new clients—major deals," he said with a dazzling smile that almost blinded her. "If I didn't know better, I might think the place really is magical."

"Congratulations twice over. That's fabulous. I assure you that the only magic involved came from your hands, heart, and brain. You must have wowed them with your ideas."

"Ready to walk the hounds?" He turned his head and grabbed the door knob.

"Am I embarrassing you, Brandon? I do think a nice ruddy color is creeping up your cheeks." Turnabout was certainly fair play and fun.

"C'mon, sunshine. Rocky needs the exercise. He's getting fat just lying around."

"Fat? I doubt it. But whatever makes you happy…"

A minute later, they were on the sand, the dogs pulling for freedom. "Nonna said I could let Sheba loose without worrying, but I won't do it when it's too dark to see into the distance." She touched his arm. "Rocky's walking so much better. You've done a really good job with him."

"Now that I have my car back, I took him to the vet today," Brandon said. "This boy is healing fast. No more plastic bag as of tomorrow."

She thought back in time for a moment. "I guess it's been an entire week, huh?" Kathy asked, glancing at the new rescue. A most handsome fellow. Then she realized what Brandon might be getting at and braced herself for disappointment.

"I haven't forgotten our deal, Brandon. Is this your way of saying you want me to take him back?"

Suddenly she was walking alone. She looked over her shoulder. Brandon had halted five steps back, but then started toward her.

"I suppose that's a fair question," he began when he stood in front of her. "But you darn well know I'm keeping him. Heck, you probably had that figured out from the get-go. So don't go all innocent on me."

"Yes!" With arms pumping, she jumped and jogged in circles on the sand. "I knew it. I knew you were a good guy right from the beginning."

He reached for her, and suddenly, she was being held snugly against his chest. "Don't give me too much credit, Katarina," he said, his voice gravelly. "Rocky knew how to soften my heart. Maybe he followed your example."

Surprise kept her silent.

"So now, a fair warning: I'm not a totally good guy, and I'm certainly not one of your brothers."

His kiss was hard, demanding, and took her breath away, before it gentled to explore her lips and mouth. Before she realized how easy it would be to go along. She pushed against his chest, and his arms loosened. She took a step back.

"The-the timing's wrong, Brandon," she said softly, her gaze steady on him. "You're not in a good place, relationship wise. And I? Well, I'd like to prove I can earn a living by working remotely full-time. And maybe, if I'm lucky…really lucky…one day the writing can come first." She paused and took a breath. "I think we both have other goals right now."

He didn't respond immediately, simply stared at her, then at the horizon, the sky, and back toward the house. "I don't believe in Bart Quinn's guff," he began, "but like Rocky, I have to put my faith in a fresh start. The beach in winter might be an unusual place to find one." He cupped his ear. "Can you hear the whoosh of the waves against the sand? Over and over since the earth began, like a lullaby. I find that comforting."

In the moonlight, she saw the peaceful planes of his face, the clearness of his eyes and heard the warmth in his voice.

"I'm doing just fine in all ways, Katarina, almost like a weight has been lifted. Maybe we'll both discover what we want here. We've got months to find out."

CHAPTER SIX

Underneath all his bluster, Brandon had a soft heart. As she made her bed the next morning, Kathy was still thinking about their conversation on the beach. Brandon certainly had shared another part of himself with her. He seemed to be reevaluating, musing on life. As for his thoughts about their surroundings...his descriptions, his reactions...well, she wouldn't have taken him for a romantic. But she did now.

On the other hand, maybe winning those two new clients had something to do with recharging his life. At the very least, it had to be a confidence builder.

She opened her refrigerator for a breakfast idea. A lot of empty space met her eye. "Whoops. I think all of Mom's care packages are gone. Today I go to the supermarket." Petting Sheba, she apologized. "I don't think they'll let you in, sweetie. You'll have to stay home."

After grabbing her purse, she ran downstairs to her car, noticing Brandon's was gone. She shrugged. Well, he didn't have to report his activities to her.

She bumped into him in the market. "Great minds and all that," she said, peering into his cart. "Lovely," she exclaimed. "Low-salt chicken soup." Her thoughts swirled. "Better yet, I can buy a bird and make a pot—enough for both of us."

"Too much trouble," he replied. "You're not here to cook, and besides—"

"I'm not the cook my mom is," she interrupted. "But soup is one staple I've learned. I can make enough for today and to freeze for later on. No problem." She tilted her head back. "Are you in?"

She saw his regret before he spoke. "Ordinarily, I would. But today, my aunt and uncle invited me for dinner. Celebrating my first week in town. Sorry."

She tamped down her initial enthusiasm. "No problem. Enjoy yourself."

"Hey…why don't you join us? I know they'll have plenty."

Socializing with strangers wasn't her bailiwick. Her supply of energy and concentration would be depleted, and she couldn't afford that. Her longed-for calm stay in this town had been challenged enough. Between the accident, the dogs, and meeting Brandon. Whew. She really needed to take back some control. "Maybe another time."

He nodded. "See you later on the beach?"

"Sure."

She prepared the soup anyway. Her idea had been last minute, and she couldn't fault him for not being available. But she was disappointed. On this Sunday evening, the apartment seemed too quiet and had her pausing to find her playlist. Music would help. In Boston, she would have been frustrated with a dozen family phone calls and the expectation of her presence at dinner with a score of people. In Pilgrim Cove, she'd be enjoying a dinner for one. Was there no happy midpoint? Maybe a dinner for two?

So, who was the romantic now?

##

As the week passed, her daily routines took shape, beginning and ending with a walk on the beach with Brandon and the canines. On a Tuesday in the middle of December, after their usual morning walk, Brandon invited her inside his apartment.

"You seem to be bringing me good luck," he said with a grin. She followed him into the kitchen and then through to the dining room where all his normal art supplies were laid bare on the extended table.

"What a lot of stuff," she said. "I thought you designed on a computer."

"I do both, but often the initial idea has me grabbing charcoal, pencils, tablets and whatever. I try to translate what I see in my head to what people can see with their eyes. You should know as a writer…when an idea excites you…you jot it down."

"I've got a pile of notebooks…sometimes too many ideas."

His deep chuckle reflected true understanding. Camaraderie. "Exactly. You develop the ones that you don't forget. It's all exercise for the brain. Nothing's wasted."

He pulled out his computer, pressed a few keys. "Every Tuesday, the big book lists come out."

"I know. *New York Times, USA Today…*" She'd educated herself well about the entire publishing industry. Now, *her* industry.

"Right," said Brandon. "Yesterday, I received an email from one of my clients—a publisher—to check out this week's lists." With a few clicks, he pulled it up and pointed. "Number one spot on both lists."

She looked, recognized the author's name immediately. "Oh, good. I loved his last one and was waiting for the next. And now it's here. I like the cover, too. Original. It kind of pulls you into the story yet leaves room for your imagination."

A beat of silence before Brandon's voice came to her. "That was my goal," he said quietly. He pulled out a carton from under the table, produced a copy of the book, and gave it to her. "A gift. Enjoy it. And don't protest—I have several more." His grin rivaled the Cheshire cat's.

"Several more?" she asked. "What's going on?"

He pressed a few keys on his computer and produced the electronic version of the cover. "My design and execution. They jumped on it." He whistled a happy note. "Good for the ego and helped my bank account, too."

Her breath caught, and her hand flew to her chest. "That's fabulous, Brandon. Congratulations. Again. Man, you're having a successful month here." While she was a very minor player in the big game of best-selling books.

"I agree. Things are coming together." His phone rang to the tune of the "Stars and Stripes Forever" march. Kathy laughed. So did Brandon. "I needed something loud."

He glanced at the readout and motioned her for quiet. But not to be gone. She sat, leaned back, and listened with curiosity as he chatted with the author, who was naturally elated and who evidently wanted Brandon to create the cover for his next book.

"Would love to do it. Have you spoken with the publisher yet?"

Brandon listened, nodded. "Yeah, I suppose they're patting themselves on the back. Well, congratulations again. I hope you achieve this success every time."

With another laugh, he hung up. "I've already been paid by his publisher, but he's sending me a case of champagne. Nice guy. But a case?"

"Maybe you'll find something else to celebrate," said Kathy, again hit by a quiver of anxiety. "To tell you the truth," she continued quietly, "I feel like I'm in an alternate universe. You rub shoulders with best-selling authors, and I'm just starting out. I-I'm a minnow in a big river." She pivoted toward the door. "I better get back to work."

"Hey. Hold on a sec."

She turned around and stared into his concerned face.

"Want some free advice?" he asked.

"Only if it's worth more than that."

"I think it is. I learned the hard way, Kat. Set your goals and stay on course. No matter what outside forces come your way." He took a breath. "You know about that bad relationship I had last year?"

She nodded. "Sort of."

"I almost lost my business, too, after growing it client by client for over five years. I allowed myself to get off track. And spent too much money also. But never again."

"No more relationships?"

"No more bad choices." He rummaged through a folder on the table. "I have something for you," he said. "Didn't think I'd ever hand it over. But now it's yours. Take a look, and don't...ever...let...me...hear the word *minnow* again."

59

Totally confused, she took the sheet of paper and glanced at the drawing.

"Does that girl look like a minor player?" he asked.

She blinked and stared at a true caricature of...herself! With her hands on hips, a headband around her dark curls, and an outraged expression, she wore a superhero costume of some kind. A sprinkling of hearts floated around her.

"Wh-What...?"

"That was you after I hit the tree. When you were fighting so hard for Rocky's future. I thought of you as an Avenger—with heart."

"Oh, my. You did? I sure don't see myself that way." She looked at the drawing again. A bit overwhelming. She peered up at him. "And I called you Uber man back then. Sorry but no pictures from me. Not even a straight line with a ruler."

"I can draw my own, and our walks on the beach are enough." He paused. "Glad I was your Uber man on that messy drive."

"That's nice to know, Brandon. I feel the same. See you tonight." She left him then and went upstairs, carefully taping the drawing to the kitchen wall, where she could see it as she worked. She'd felt safe following him on that "messy drive." This gift he'd given her was more than a drawing. It reflected how he'd seen her. A Supergirl. And now he'd shared it so she would believe in herself. Which she normally did, but he didn't know that.

I am not one of your brothers.

The words popped into her mind as she remembered their kiss on the beach a couple of weeks ago. It seemed Brandon had come to terms with past mistakes, had no lingering regrets, and was focused on the future.

She idly wondered how she'd react if Brandon kissed her again, but dismissed the thought immediately. She had no time for a personal romance. Much better to focus on *A Calculated Incident* and Dana Moretti's problems in solving a murder. Hadn't Brandon told her to keep her eye on the prize? Maybe Dana would meet the right man one day. And maybe Kathy would be able to afford a cover designed by Brandon Bigelow.

The next morning started with a phone call from Boston. "I'll be home for Christmas Day, Mom. I promise. And I'll bake plenty of cookies—yes, the ones I actually know how to make. Hey, I miss you, too, but I'm really happy here. Nonna did me a great favor."

Kathy listened to her mom's admonitions, heard the concern and love in her voice. "Love you, too, Mom. Always. We'll see you next Wednesday."

Her mom interrupted. "Who's we?"

Kathy replied, bewildered. "Sheba and me, of course!"

She disconnected and paused. Okay. She had to admit that family ties pulled a bit. Maybe because it was holiday time and her memories of annual traditions tugged at her heart. Maybe because she knew that in and around all the noise was woven a ribbon of love.

Feeling more content, she went back to her computer and her insurance company projects, the employment that paid her real salary. In moments, she was deeply engrossed, and when she glanced at the time later on, hours had flown by. She sighed contentedly, checked in with her boss, and hung up satisfied. She supposed most people would be bored with these types of assignments, but she enjoyed working the numbers, the percentages, her fingers as nimble with spreadsheets as with a Word document.

"Want to go out, Sheb?"

The dog was instantly on her feet and at Kathy's side.

"We need a break. At least I need a break. All you do is sleep. Such a good girl." Sheba kissed her and danced around Kathy as though she were the only star in her orbit.

Kathy zipped up her parka and attached Sheba's leash. "Let's go."

To her surprise, Brandon and Rocky were waiting at her downstairs door. His eyes seemed to shine when he saw her.

"I was just on my way up," he said, "and here you are."

"Anything special on your mind?"

He threw his head back, then looked at her. "Oh, there are a few special things on my mind, but right now, only one. Another rescue. Rather, multiple rescues. I'll tell you while we walk these guys. Only a short walk this time."

Her curiosity grew as they headed down the driveway to the street. "What are you talking about? Multiple rescues?" Then recent memories clicked, and she knew the issue before Brandon explained.

"Adam Fielding called me. He needs help. That lady they were talking about—Rita Murray—well, her son is involved now. Whatever her future living arrangements may be...she can't have those dogs."

"About time the son showed up."

Brandon waited a moment, tracked Rocky's activities, then turned back to her. "Listen up, Katarina."

She paid attention, having noted his use of her full name. He seemed to do that for important things.

"Fielding can't handle this mission alone because—and wait for this—his wife's having a baby. Maybe today. I'm not sure."

"Oh, my goodness. Everything always happens at once." Her mind raced. "How about an animal rescue center—if they have one in this town."

"Fielding *is* the rescue center around here. He started by rescuing retired greyhounds. Remember, I wrote a check to *Greys and Strays.*"

"Right." She nodded in agreement. "I remember—now that you reminded me—but how about the ROMEOs? I thought they take care of this town. Did you call your uncle?"

He shook his head. "Good idea, but I came straight to you. I imagine they'll help but, Kat, the vet may have called me, but he really called us." He took a deep breath. "Do you want to embody the lady in my drawing again?"

The question stunned and amused her simultaneously. Did he really see her as a superhero? An Avenger? She couldn't let him down. Besides, she'd never turn her back on helping rescues.

"A couple of things," she began as they retraced their steps. "Our own dogs stay home. The others might have ticks and fleas and God knows what else."

He stepped backwards, and the look on his face…priceless.

"But there's medicine for that," she reassured. "You don't know much about animals, I guess."

"You guess right. Didn't have a dog growing up."

"But it's never too late. You're a natural."

Like a little boy, he grinned at her praise, and she had to laugh. She squeezed his arm. "You really are a softie inside. I like that."

"Dogs are easier than humans. They're honest."

##

The vet's waiting room seemed brimming with people when Kathy and Brandon arrived, but it was the brunette in the wheelchair who smiled up and greeted them as though she weren't about to give birth imminently. As though it were a sunshiny day.

"Hello and thank you. I'm Becca, who usually assists Peggy in running this office. But Peggy's sick." Suddenly, she winced.

Kathy stared, not breathing herself. "Is the doc in the back? I'll get him."

"Wait," said Brandon, whose complexion had paled. "I'll get him...and stay there."

Kathy pushed him toward the examining room. "Go, go." She went to Becca. "What can I do?"

A blonde woman spoke up. "I'm Lila Parker. My daughter and Sara are best friends and the girls are with Adam now." She waved toward where Brandon had disappeared. "I'm also Bart Quinn's granddaughter and partner. I'm very sorry for not visiting you at Sea View House yet."

"That's okay. I'm usually working anyway."

Becca stretched her hand out. "Then special thanks for stepping in. Adam told me all about the accident and the rescue you guys did. That was amazing, and I'm sorry I missed all the excitement."

"Well, you're making up for it now!"

"Yeah, I'm good at that," Becca said. "I figure if I survived a bombing, I'll survive childbirth, too."

That sounded like a story, but for another time. Kathy looked from Lila to Becca. "First, please give me your cell numbers. And then tell me the plan."

"We're leaving Sara and Katie with you," said Becca. "I told Sara she was in charge. That child actually knows quite a lot about tending to the patients."

"Quite a lot?" echoed Lila. "The kid is half a vet already. So smart. And my daughter...well, she's always up for an adventure." The woman's laugh sparkled in the air, and Kathy felt like joining in. "I'll be in touch about picking the kids up for the night."

She leaned over to kiss Becca. "Good luck, my friend. I'll be waiting to hear. But now, I've got to get back to the little boss." The woman left in a cloud of goodwill and laughter.

"She means her other daughter—a two-year-old," said Becca, handing Kathy a slip of paper with phone numbers.

"I'm going to enter them in my phone right now before I lose this."

Children's voices approached, and Kathy saw Sara and blonde Katie come into the room. Sara ran toward her mom, reached around her, and leaned in. "Love you, Mom."

"And I love you. Where's your dad?"

"Right here. Are we ready?"

In thirty seconds, the place was quiet. An eerie contrast, which must have hit Sara hard. The girl started crying, her words broken and full of worry. "What if something bad happens? Like to my first mom. And my Becca, who I love so much, almost died once already. Why couldn't I go with them?"

Stunned, Kathy gulped and blinked back tears, but before she could say a word, she heard Brandon's voice.

"You couldn't go, Sara, because you're needed here. You already know it's the best way you can help your folks."

Sara whirled toward him. Her big brown eyes shone with tears as she stared at the man who'd rescued Rocky.

"We have eight rescues back there that need attention," said Brandon in a quiet, calm voice, "and your staff here is waiting for directions."

"Pretend you really are Dr. Sara," said Katie.

Sara rubbed the tears away and stood straighter. "Follow me."

Each dog was in his own kennel. "They have water, but they need baths, they need food. And we'll see what else. One at a time, people." Dr. Sara's orders.

Kathy glanced at Brandon and gave him a thumbs-up. He answered with a grin and head shake.

"We'll label the cages and dogs with matching numbers and make sure each rescue goes into his or her proper cage. Some of them look alike." She peered up at Brandon. "A couple look like Rocky."

"Oh, no, Doc. Don't go there. One is enough for me."

Two hours of hard work led to more. "They have roundworms," said Sara after examining the evidence. "What was that Mrs. Murray thinking? These pups need attention and good homes. Every one of them."

Brandon took out his wallet. "I don't care what anyone says, I'm putting out a call for the ROMEOs. For all we know, maybe a couple of them would adopt one of these guys or gals. And that's the point, isn't it?"

He called his uncle and summed up the situation. "If you can get on the horn to all your friends, and let them know." He looked at Kathy with an odd expression. "He wants to know if they're adorable."

"What?"

"Says it's a selling point."

"Of course they're adorable," said Sara. "At least they will be by the time we get finished with them. If Papa Bart were here, he'd know what to do." The look she gave Brandon definitely relegated him to second place.

"Uncle Ralph says you're right," Brandon offered. "And that Bart's coming home for Christmas next week."

"He is?" asked Katie, jumping into the conversation. "Nobody told me. Nobody tells me anything! Just wait till I see…"

Uh-oh. Kathy saw the uncomfortable expression on Brandon's face. "I think you might get Brandon in trouble if you spill those beans," she said to Katie. "It was probably a surprise for you."

"Oh." She offered Brandon a wide smile. "Then I won't say anything." She stepped closer toward her friend. "And now you don't have to worry, Sara. Papa Bart will figure it out."

Sara's grin reflected her relief…for a moment. She turned toward Kathy. "Did my dad call you yet?"

Oh, baby. Kathy didn't remember ever having the kind of real-life issues this youngster had. "My cell's been quiet so far. Maybe your new sibling is so happy where he or she is that…"

Sara gave her an incredulous stare. "Or maybe my mom needs some Pitocin to get that baby going. It's no good if the delivery takes forever."

Brandon shot her an amazed glance. Kathy returned it. This was definitely the most intense babysitting job she'd ever taken on.

"Or maybe," Sara continued, "the baby's turned around. Breech. I once helped Dad deliver a calf and that's what happened. He had to reach in and turn that baby around to get him out."

"And maybe the sky is going to fall…but not today," said Kathy firmly. "These rescues need our attention. Remember? That's our job. What's next, Sara?"

The girl nodded and resumed her caretaking role. Eight undernourished pups.

"It's hard to believe that Rocky once looked like that," said Kathy. "And it's been how long, Brandon?"

"Hmm. About three weeks, I think. It's amazing."

"It almost feels like a lifetime…" she murmured.

His eyes focused on her. "Is that good or bad?" he asked softly.

"I haven't decided. But one thing I do know for sure," she replied, searching for each word. "There are as many distractions in 'quiet' Pilgrim Cove as there ever were at home." She felt the warmth rise to her neck and cheeks and avoided his eyes.

"So, I'll ask the same question. Are distractions good or bad?" His voice was tinged with more than curiosity. As though her answer mattered.

She snuck a quick peek at his face. Yeah, he looked a little uncertain. "My answer is the same, too. I haven't decided yet."

The office phone rang, and like a flash of lightning, Sara was on it. "Really? Really?" Squeals and tears. She looked at the others. "I have a baby brother! And Mom can't wait to get home."

Kathy sank into the nearest chair. Brandon took out his cell phone and started taking pictures. "For their family album," he said, nodding toward Sara. "Her folks will enjoy what they've missed here."

Typical graphic artist? Typical thirtysomething? Or a thoughtful man? A social guy who cared about others. His actions reinforced her prior thoughts about him. He'd left his past experience behind and was moving on. She heartily approved of the emerging Brandon, the real Brandon Bigelow.

CHAPTER SEVEN

They were back in the vet's office the next morning, taking care of the orphaned pups. Adam had checked every one of them while Sara slept late. Fortunately, Becca's mom was on her way to town from the western part of the state and would arrive soon.

"Thank goodness for grandmas," said Kathy. "I'm crazy about mine."

"Oh, I'm happy she's coming, but you guys have been incredible, too," said the vet. "Vaccinations for your guys are on the house from now on."

Brandon grinned. "Well...let's be honest. That was some phone call yesterday. You gave us no choice but to show up."

"There are always choices," Adam replied. "But I knew you'd come through. Sea View House tenants never disappoint." He checked his watch. "I'll get Sara up and take her with me to see her mom. Relieve some anxiety."

The man disappeared without another word.

"Well, I guess that's that and here we are again," said Kathy. "The two least experienced dog handlers in the entire town."

"You've got that right."

She approached the second kennel and lifted out a pretty girl. "She could be Rocky's sister." She stroked her and examined her paws. "No major abrasions on this one, but I can feel her ribs. Oh, you poor baby." She sat down and snuggled her close, murmuring love words.

"Be careful, Kat. I think you're falling…"

She sat perfectly still, his words registering. Would adopting a rescue really be a bad thing? "Sheba's mine only for a few months," she whispered.

Brandon selected another dog and started to feed him by hand. "Think about it for a moment," he said. "Boston's different from Pilgrim Cove. No beach, no easy access in and out the house. You probably live in an apartment three stories up."

He'd nailed it. "And what about you?" she challenged. "Same thing for you."

He was quiet for a moment. "I'll be looking for a new place," he finally said, "and it occurred to me that I'm not married to Boston. I can live and work anywhere."

He kept silent then, and as Kathy stared at him, the proverbial coin dropped. "Are you thinking what I think you're thinking?"

"It's a possibility. Not Sea View House, of course, but there must be others to rent. And I found out that Boston's only thirty minutes by commuter ferry. People go back and forth all year round."

"I had no idea. You are way ahead of me. I'm still getting through one day at a time here. And sometimes…struggling." As soon as the words slipped out of her mouth, she wanted to retract them. Why in the world had she shared her concerns with Brandon?

His brow furrowed, and his eyes narrowed. "Why the struggle?"

"There have been so many interruptions!" She inhaled deeply. Then exhaled. "Now I feel better. I just had to let that out."

"It's all about the writing, isn't it?"

How did he know? "My insurance work comes first. That takes at least thirty hours. I enjoy it and get paid well. But…"

"The writing gets short shrift," he finished, "and despite your being a genius math person, creating a complete novel is harder."

"Seems to be. Except for the first week, so far, this-this Pilgrim Cove experiment isn't working for me the way I'd hoped."

"Let me know how I can help," he said. "We creatives need to be there for one another, have each other's backs. It's not an easy way to make a living."

He understood and that was enough. "Hey Uber man, you don't have to rescue me again or"—she giggled—"was it the other way around? I forget."

His eyes gleamed. "We are quite a team, Katarina. But here's something to hang on to. I work twenty-four seven on one career. You're trying to juggle two."

"Thank you, Brandon. You've helped me already. And if I weren't caring for this sweet pup, I'd give you a big hug."

"I'll definitely take a rain check."

She'd look forward to it.

Friday stretched out before Kathy, seemingly as a much-hoped-for normal day. A concept that had become as elusive as four-leaf clovers. No more puppies to tend to, no more emotional moments with a child who shouldn't have had to bear them, no more upside-down schedules, which meant no schedule at all. Today she'd restart her use of time.

Brandon had been correct. She was working two jobs, but only one paid the bills. There had been a time, years ago, when she'd imagined a university career teaching math or statistics and studying for a doctorate. It hadn't happened. She'd been surrounded by truly brilliant graduate students, the caliber of minds that MIT and Harvard attracted. She hadn't been an A-lister.

She started her computer and logged on to her current project—determining life insurance charges for young parents. Hmm. She'd met a few young parents in Pilgrim Cove already. People just like Lila and Becca were in her mind as she continued her work to determine risk factors for this group, such as recreational activities. Rock climbing anyone?

The sharp knock and Brandon's voice came to her, breaking her concentration. "Come on down. We've got company."

I'm busy! But she rose, stretched, and turned her head left and right a few times, stretching her neck. She glanced at the clock. Good Lord. It was afternoon. "Sheba, let's go for a walk."

A minute later, Kathy stood in front of Bart Quinn with his beaming smile and white thatch of thick hair uncovered.

The man extended his hand. "Hello, Katarina Russo! I bring you greetings and love from your grandma, who says you should call more often."

In his Irish leprechaun mode. Definitely. Sheba pulled the leash. "Mr. Quinn—either come with me to the curb, or go inside. It's cold out here." She started walking but turned back. "And by the way, I call Nonna at least twice a week!"

His hearty laughter followed as she waited for Sheba to finish up. Nice that young Katie didn't have to keep a secret anymore.

They congregated in Brandon's kitchen. "Can't stay too long," said Bart. "A lot of happenings behind my back, so I've got visits to make."

Kathy would bet nothing escaped his knowledge in this town. He looked from her to Brandon. "Is Sea View House not what I promised? With the beach, the ocean...winter can be good, too." He leaned down to pet Rocky. "And this young man's come to join you. Good, good. Life is good." He sat down at the table, and the others joined him.

"You kept your promise, Bart Quinn," said Brandon. "The house is perfect, the ocean is majestic, and my upstairs neighbor made sure Rocky found a home."

"Ach, there's that. I hear you met by accident, I did." His eyes twinkled as though he'd delivered the most unique joke. "Couldn't even wait to arrive at this beauty here and feel the magic."

"I'm ignoring that," said Brandon. "You can't stay away from this town for long, can you? It's only a month since you left, and now you're back for Christmas, I was told."

"You bet. What's a holiday without my family? But Honey stayed down south with Teresa right next door. They'll be fine." He leaned in. "We do FaceTime, you know," he whispered, his eyelids closed for a moment. "Ahh...I should give credit. My Honeybelle figured it out, and now my young Katie and I can visit. She's a marvel, she is."

He took out his wallet and addressed them both. "Have you kept the special ROMEO card? My pals will take care of you if you run into trouble. Call Ralph Bigelow if the lights go out."

Brandon chuckled.

"I certainly hope they don't," said Kathy, "but my card is in the top kitchen drawer just in case. Thanks."

The man started to rise. "Almost forgot. I'll see you tomorrow night at the Lobster Pot. Dinner at seven. The best food along the entire coast, and it's on the house. My daughters own it, and Ralph and Linda will be there, too."

Totally bewildered, Kathy looked at Brandon. "Did you know…?"

But her neighbor was laughing while shaking his head. "You look like you fell down the rabbit hole and landed on a toadstool. I probably looked exactly the same when I met the whole crew in the diner last month. A real experience."

He certainly seemed to be enjoying life in Pilgrim Cove. Well, she had other things to do. "I'm sorry, Mr. Quinn. Thanks for the invite, but I can't make it."

"A Saturday night?" said Quinn. "Ohh—do you have a date?" He glanced at Brandon, his eyebrows squishing together.

"With her latest book, most likely," said Brandon.

She took a breath. "Exactly right. Time is passing. Your quiet little town, Mr. Quinn, is not as quiet as you might think. I have only two more months on this lease, and almost nothing has been accomplished!"

Quinn's eyes almost popped from his head. "Lease? Who said anything about a lease?"

"I signed one."

He waved that away. "Pooh. It's flexible. I'm the one in charge, aren't I? The William Adams Foundation gets the money no matter who's renting. So problem solved. Stay longer." He waved and walked toward his car. "See you tomorrow night at seven!"

##

At six thirty the next evening, Kathy searched her closet floor for the tall black leather boots she'd brought with her in case she'd have an occasion like this. A dinner out. Despite her initial nonchalance, she found a tad of excitement growing and chalked it up to a change of pace. She'd been living in grunge outfits for almost a month. Clean, for sure. But it was about time to change out of sweats and comfy jeans, at least for a little while.

Brandon had insisted on picking her up at her apartment. "And don't argue," he'd said. So, she hadn't, but thought it was silly when she could have just walked downstairs. It wasn't a real date. It was a Bart Quinn command performance.

She stood and adjusted the high-heeled boots, straightened her mid-calf-length black skirt, and pushed up the sleeves of her red turtleneck sweater. Hopefully, she was put together. The Crow's Nest was definitely in need of a full-length mirror. But she paused in front of the small one in the bathroom to add a gold chain round her neck and gold button earrings. Her wavy hair hung loose past her shoulders. Probably needed a cut. She shrugged. Whatever. She'd have to do.

She heard a knock followed by Brandon's voice, and she rushed to the door. "I'm ready," she said as she opened it.

His eyes widened as his gaze roamed from her head to feet. "Wow. You're always cute, but tonight…" He let his voice drift.

"You mean I clean up pretty well?" she blustered while feeling heat creep up her neck. "I'd really prefer a run on the beach instead of being thrown into a crowd of people I don't know."

His eyebrows rose, and a slow smile appeared. "You know me."

True. "You're one person."

"Who won't leave your side all night. I guarantee you'll know everyone by the time the evening's over."

It really made no difference to her if she did or didn't. Brandon could have fit right into her family, drawing energy from being with others.

They descended the stairs and walked to the SUV. "I wouldn't have expected you to be a shy superhero," he said when he opened the door and waited for her to get in.

"Oh, I can fake it," she said with a laugh. "I just take a deep breath, walk in, and count the minutes until I can leave."

"I don't think you're going to escape too quickly tonight. But if you relax, you can have some fun and enjoy a great meal." He slammed her door shut.

Enjoy a meal? If her stomach would unknot, maybe he'd be right. She leaned back as he got behind the wheel and threw a manila envelope onto the back seat.

"A glass of wine might help," she said.

"You've got it," he said as the car roared to life. "As many as you want."

"Just one glass gets my legs dancing, and that's all I need."

She smiled at him, and his eyes darkened. Their gaze held like a pair of magnets unable to separate. A shiver of desire coursed through her. Totally unexpected, unlooked for. But also…exciting.

"I-I think you'd better start driving," she said, her voice unnaturally low.

He checked behind him and backed up. "That killer smile," he said, "can drop a man to his knees."

His words rang a bell. *A killer smile.* That's how he saw her. That's how he'd captured her alter ego on paper. A unique vision.

"I'm not nervous about dinner anymore."

His laughter filled the car. "Glad I gave you something else to think about."

As soon as they walked through the front doors of the Lobster Pot and inhaled the aroma of clam chowder, freshly baked fish, and a variety of seafood, Kathy's stomach rumbled.

The hostess flashed a grin. "I heard that! It happens all the time."

"Good to know, but it really does smell delicious in here. And look at that cute sign." She pointed toward a wall behind the hostess stand, where a brightly colored poster proclaimed: *Don't Mussel Your Way In!*

"Cute," said Brandon. "And sends a message. Graphic design at its best. I happen to enjoy puns."

"Me, too."

"Ahoy, my friends," came a familiar voice. "Right on time." Quinn waved them over. "Your aunt and uncle are already here. My friend Sam Parker and his family from the hardware store, too. And of course, my own clan. Follow me." The man's eyes softened as he looked ahead to a group of tables set up for them in an alcove of the main dining room. A bustling dining room.

As they approached the group, and before Kathy had a chance to steel herself, young Katie Parker skipped over to greet them. Then she whirled to face the others in their party. "Hey, everybody. Here are the people who helped Sara and me save Mrs. Murray's dogs while Ms.

Becca had a baby. And Mr. Brandon adopted one of them."

"A dog, not a baby," said Brandon, saluting the crowd.

Before the girl could say another word, the group erupted into spontaneous applause.

"Where's my glass of wine?" whispered Kathy. "This is terrible."

"Soon, soon," replied Brandon, leading her to the seats next to Linda and Ralph, who welcomed them warmly.

"It's such a treat that Brandon's been living here, and now we've met his neighbor, too," said Linda. "You're welcome to our home anytime."

Kathy's heart softened. The woman reminded her of her own mom. "Open-door policy, huh?"

"Of course. In this town, there couldn't be anything else, right, everyone?"

A chorus responded. Their camaraderie reflected the comfort of longtime friends—of course a generation older than she—but Kathy recognized their sincerity. The real thing.

Lila waved and came over to chat, revealing that all was well in the Fielding household now. "Sara is so thrilled with her new brother, she turned down our dinner invitation tonight.

"I'm glad she's happy," said Kathy. "It was a rough couple of days for her."

"For you guys, too," said Lila. "Well, we all know that Sea View House attracts great people, but you two really came through for our friends." She raised a glass. "Hear, hear."

With all eyes on them, Kathy wanted to crawl under the table. She'd never sought the spotlight in her life. Brandon must have sensed her unease. His hand engulfed hers immediately. She wrapped her fingers around his. "Smile," he whispered. "Wave. In ten seconds, it'll be over. Your wine is waiting for you."

He was right about both.

Brandon's aunt had a sharp eye. "Sorry about all that attention, but their salute to you is honest and heartfelt."

Kathy smiled at her. "I know. I just prefer being behind the scenes, not starring in one...if you know what I mean."

"I do, indeed. I wasn't born here, you know. But Ralph"—she reached for her husband's hand—"he loved his hometown. It took a little convincing for this Boston girl, but everything worked out perfectly in the end."

Nice story, but not Kathy's story. "Good. I like happy endings."

"There are a lot of those besides ours in this town. Lots of heartache, too. No matter how Bart talks up this place like it's paradise on earth, in the end, it's real enough."

"No magic spells or fairy godmothers?" Kathy teased.

Linda paused. "Well...I wouldn't exactly say that. There's always a little magic in the air."

"Uncle! I'm crying uncle," said Kathy, appealing to Brandon, who was laughing and shaking his head.

"I'm done with that topic. Here's another." He pointed toward a poster on a nearby wall. "Take a look. There are cartoons everywhere."

Kathy stared at a caricature of a little boy holding a fishing pole. The caption said: *Wouldn't you rudder be fishing?*

No comment.

"Look at that one." Brandon pointed toward a school of fish in the ocean. The caption: *Our fish go to the best schools!*

"Okay, okay. I've had enough," said Kathy. "Cute but corny. Who comes up with these things?"

Ralph looked over toward them. "We get a kick out of them—usually. It's Bart's daughters who make them up, Thea and Maggie. They own the good ship Lobster Pot. Maggie's Lila's mom, little Katie's grandma."

"You should all have been wearing name tags," said Kathy.

A blonde woman walked toward them at a fast clip, her resemblance to Lila striking. "Welcome, welcome. Sorry I wasn't at the door to greet you. I'm Maggie Sullivan, and I hope you'll enjoy every morsel." She looked at Brandon. "Remember, it's on the house."

"Oh, no," said Kathy. "I couldn't…I'd rather…"

"Special for first timers living at Sea View House," said Maggie. "It's a tradition."

"I swear, sometimes I feel I'm in another dimension," said Kathy.

Brandon leaned over and whispered loud enough to be heard: "She wants to make sure you come back."

Maggie chuckled and extended her hand, palm up. "What do you have for me, Brandon Bigelow?"

He reached for the manila envelope he'd placed on the floor and pulled out two sheets of stock drawing paper with photos of the rescued dogs lined across the center in two rows. Three above and four below.

"Add them to your wall collection, Ms. Maggie," said Brandon, "but I suggest hanging one in the entryway."

Maggie studied the poster for a moment, her eyebrows raised. "Take a look, everyone. These pups will find a home soon." She held up one poster in each hand, facing the crowd.

Kathy stretched to see. Across the top were beautifully hand-printed words that said: *Get a New*

Leash on Life! Beneath the rescues, Brandon had written: *See our vet to adopt your pet! (Adam Fielding)*

"Oh, Brandon. This is beautiful. You took those shots from your cell phone and turned them into…into, I don't know, works of art, I guess."

His neck turned ruddy. "The computer did all the work. I've got a few more at the house to distribute down Main Street. Want to help me?"

The town was sucking her in again, but she couldn't refuse him. Such a good guy. "Sure."

Bart Quinn stood up with his glass in hand. "I'm saluting our new tenants once more, and I'm cheering for myself. Bart Quinn still goes with his gut and knows how to pick winners."

The servers came with clam chowder for everyone. The aroma had Kathy salivating. She dipped her spoon in and brought it to her mouth. "Ambrosia," she muttered. "Delicious."

"And now you can finally relax and enjoy yourself," said Brandon. "Everyone's focused on feeding their bellies."

She smiled at him. "I hope so."

"They're good people, Katarina, and you are, too. You fit right in."

She gazed around the room, the tables full of folks enjoying themselves, the walls dotted with homegrown corny posters penned by fabulous chefs, and Brandon, who now leaned back in his chair, totally relaxed and looking as if he'd confirmed for himself their prior conversation at the vet's office.

He was the one who fit right in. He had found his new home.

CHAPTER EIGHT

Holding hands seemed natural as they walked back to the car after dinner. Kathy was the first to speak. "Okay. I admit I had a good time—in the end."

"Wasn't worried for a second." Brandon's deep laughter sent a tingle through her.

"You don't really know me very well," she protested. "How could you be so sure?"

They'd reached his SUV and Brandon unlocked the passenger door, then turned toward her. "Because you always step up to the plate when the going gets tough. I know you better than you think, and I believe in you more than you do yourself. I'll stop now, but I guess that's enough for the moment." He opened her door. "Get in before you freeze."

Between the warmth, curiosity, and a wee frisson of anger he'd ignited, freezing was out of the question. She sat down and looked ahead, recognizing a few diners leaving the restaurant. Brandon would know them all in a little while. A new beginning for a confident guy, even after his recent upheavals.

As soon as he got behind the wheel, she said, "If I didn't believe in myself, Brandon, I'd walk away from the writing in a heartbeat. I've conjured up enough plots for a lifetime, but do you have any idea of the effort I've put in? The seminars, workshops, and classes I've attended to hone the craft? All while working full-time at my day job? It hasn't been easy, but I love it."

He started the engine and let the car warm up. "I really got to you, huh?"

"Don't start playing shrink with me…" she warned.

"Not guilty," he said as he began to drive. "Only one psych course in my life. But I understand this—nothing worthwhile is easy. You know the old joke about overnight success taking only twenty years to achieve? That's the story of most artists and writers."

She paused to think. "Yeah, I've actually heard that joke many times. Unfortunately, it can knock the wind out of a writer just getting started."

He turned from Main Street onto Outlook Drive. "And then you get over it. I'll bet when you held that first published book in your hand—what was it again? Oh, *A Foul Day on Campus*— all the aggravation disappeared." He glanced over at her. "Other authors have told me finishing a book is like giving birth. Even the men agreed, although how they'd know what that's like, I can't say."

She twisted in her seat belt, excited. "But they're all exactly right. I ordered a dozen copies of the print version, and when they arrived…reality hit so hard I almost keeled over. And then I danced. I danced around my apartment for a long time. It really was like having a baby."

His amused expression made her smile. "Did it take nine months to cook?" he asked.

"Every minute of it and more."

He pulled into their driveway. "We're home," he announced.

She glanced at him in surprise. "What?"

He waved toward the big house. "I guess that sounded funny," he said, getting out of the car, "but it's true."

She met him outside. "A temporary home," she clarified.

"Details, details…"

He opened her apartment door and stepped into the vestibule. "I had a great time tonight, Kat, and it had nothing to do with Quinn and company."

"I did, too. Despite Quinn and company." She looked into his face and saw the smoky heat in his eyes. "How did you know the title of my book?" she whispered. "I don't think I've ever mentioned it."

"Your website," he replied, his voice husky. "A copy of it is in my e-reader now."

"Really?"

"Really. I like mysteries, Katarina…"

He leaned toward her, and his lips captured hers in a deliberate, slow, thoughtful kiss. The hunger in her response surprised her, and his kiss immediately turned more demanding. She parted her lips and tasted his wine-sweetened tongue. Nice, perfect. She tilted her head back farther and felt his arm go around her.

"I knew it would be like this," he whispered as he nibbled on her earlobe. "I couldn't take my eyes from you all night."

"I noticed," she whispered. "Which is why I kept turning pink."

"Not the wine then?" he teased.

"No, not the wine." It was Brandon. His humor, talent, friendliness, and most of all, his generous heart. She cupped his cheek, needing to touch. To extend the connection for a moment. He stood quietly at first, then gently took her hand and kissed her palm, causing a shiver to race through her.

She hadn't been looking for a relationship at all when she came to Pilgrim Cove. She hadn't been looking for one in Boston, either. When the right man came along…she'd know it. At least, she'd thought so. Just like Nonna had known when she met Kathy's granddad.

She took a step back, and he released her at once. "I think we're being called." She pointed to their respective doors, where they could hear the dogs barking. "See you in a few."

"I'll be waiting."

##

Saturday night had changed everything. In the three days since their dinner at the Lobster Pot, Brandon seemed to be perched in the back of Kathy's mind, or on her shoulder. Or on her kitchen chair eating lunch! Although she'd been as busy as always with her work, her thoughts constantly returned to him.

She finished packing her overnight bag for her Christmas visit home and gathered Sheba's paraphernalia. Her homemade Christmas cookies came next. She put aside a handful for Brandon and wrapped the rest in layers of aluminum foil.

"I'll be right back for you, Sheba. Gotta start loading the car, and then we'll say goodbye to Brandon and Rocky."

She received a lick and a whine in response. Kathy kneeled in front of the dog and hugged her. "You are the best. I'll miss you when Nonna comes back."

A knock was followed by a "Hello in there."

She unlocked the door for Brandon, who took a look at her activities and frowned. "Why don't I just drive you into Boston?"

"Is the weather forecast bad?" asked Kathy. "I really haven't been listening."

"Not too bad, but…you've got the dog, and a lot on your mind…"

"And you think I'm a lousy driver," joked Kathy.

"Never said that. Our trip down here took twice as long as it should have and the conditions were really bad. But I don't mind being Uber man again."

She gave him a hug. "Thanks, Bran, but I've got this." She couldn't contemplate him meeting her three brothers right now, not to mention her folks. Much too soon.

He stared at her for a long minute. "You have nothing to prove to me, but I'll expect a phone call as soon as you arrive." He began pacing the room. "Too bad my folks are coming here, and you have to go there." He took her in his arms. "If you run into any kind of road trouble, you call me."

She nestled closer. "Aye, aye, captain."

"Smart aleck." He leaned over, and when his mouth touched hers, she didn't want to leave at all.

###

Even Rocky missed her. Or it might have been Sheba he missed. Not only was walking the beach lonely, but the Captain's Quarters wasn't the same with an empty apartment upstairs. Brandon missed the sound of life that had come to him through the walls or doors. True to her word, Kat had called when she'd reached Boston, and Brandon had exhaled a breath of relief he hadn't know he'd been holding. She also promised to call when she left town the day after Christmas. He had to be content with that, but a phone call wasn't the same as her real presence.

His folks had arrived the night before, and they'd all gone to church together, including his aunt and uncle. He'd earned an atta boy for that. He'd thought going would be a good distraction, but it turned out to be more than that as people he'd already met greeted him like a long-lost friend after the service. His parents were impressed—and happy.

"You are looking good, sounding good, and the spring is back in your step," said his dad. "Must be some magic in the air."

"Ha! More like the magic at Sea View House," said his aunt.

"And that's my cue to get on home. See you tomorrow." He'd waved and got into his car.

Now, he and Rocky jogged back to the house on Christmas morning with nothing on the agenda until dinner at his relatives' later that day. He went inside and, by force of habit, went to his computer, checking up on a new project he'd started designing the day before. Ten minutes later, he gave up. Couldn't concentrate, which was unusual. He stood, stretched, and spotted his e-reader at the other end of the table. Perfect! Reading Kat's book would be as close to being with her as possible until she returned the next day.

"Next year, paper plates!" Kathy joked to her mom as she loaded the last glass into the dishwasher.

"We say that every year, but it doesn't happen," replied Marie, drying her hands with a dish towel. "A holiday table should be special."

Kathy's cell phone interrupted. She glanced at the readout, happy to see the caller's name. "Gotta take this one, Mom," she said and scampered to a quiet place near the top of the stairs leading to the second floor of the colonial-style house.

"Hey, Brandon—"

"Dana Moretti, I presume?"

Her professor detective. "You read it?" Her heart started thumping so hard she thought it would explode from her chest. *Keep cool, keep cool.* "Do you like mysteries?"

"Definitely. Both real and fictional. Nice job, Katarina Russo-Dana Moretti. You kept me guessing almost to the end."

"That's just what I wanted to hear! Thank you. And you were very perceptive about my alter ego." She trusted him now, trusted him enough to share a creative secret. "Dana is me on another road, a road I really wanted but didn't quite have the chops for."

"Detective?"

"Nope. Mathematics professor."

She heard a long, low whistle come through the phone. "I wouldn't have guessed. You seem very happy with what you're doing now."

"The forsaken college career is old news. And you're right. I'm very happy with my life now."

"Well, we can't have that, Katarina. So here comes a curve ball."

She knew that writers needed a thick skin to take criticism, and braced herself. "I'm listening."

"Your story is much better than the cover suggests, and frankly, your website stinks. You'd better work on that so readers will want to visit you online."

He made a good point, one that had been niggling at her for a while. But she had no time to fix it; design was not really in her wheelhouse. "You know what they say about being a jack of all trades and a master of none?"

"I've heard that more than once in my life."

"That would be me if I tried to learn another skill set." However, she knew someone who already had all those skills. She took a deep breath, crossed her fingers, and hoped he'd go along with her new idea. "So I'm going to offer you the deal of a lifetime." She heard him chuckle at the other end.

"This should be interesting. I'm listening."

"I will cook dinner for you every night we're at Sea View House in exchange for a website redesign"—she might as well go for broke here—"and a book cover for the second release, the one I'm working on now, *A Calculated Incident.*"

Brandon didn't answer right away, and she gripped the phone tightly. The man probably had no time, either, with all the due dates for his own work facing him.

"No fair," he said. "You told me you couldn't cook, so I might be on the losing end of this deal. Let's see…how did the cookies go over with your folks? Anyone on the floor in a stupor?"

All that stress for nothing. "Stop it! I'm not that bad." She peered under the banister. "I'm looking for the plate now…and guess what? It's almost empty."

"The background noise is very reassuring."

"They're still alive, but if I stay on the phone any longer, they're going to start asking questions I don't want to answer. So, do we have a deal?"

"I'm still thinking about it. I figure if you cooked every night, we'd be eating cereal by Saturday. So here's my counteroffer: you get weekends off. We'll figure something out."

Her entire body collapsed like broken rubber bands. "Thanks, Brandon. I really appreciate it. I do know how important a good website is."

"My pleasure. One day, you'll pay it forward to someone else."

Interesting idea. "Like you're doing now?"

"Exactly." He paused. "So you really owe me nothing. No strings, Katarina. No strings attached."

"Cooking for you will be my pleasure—I think. See you tomorrow."

##

She looked through the stiles of the staircase, her eyes resting on her dad, mom, each of her brothers, one sister-in-law, and a couple of aunts and uncles and cousins. A typical Russo full house. Actually, it had been a nice day, full of love and noise, of course, plus lots of attention for Sheba, who stayed close to Kathy when she realized Nonna wasn't there. Kathy rubbed behind the dog's ears now. "I'd never leave you behind, girl. Never."

She ran down the stairs and started for her mom.

"So who were you on the phone with for so long?" asked Joey, her oldest brother. Instantly, all eyes focused on her.

Anger flared inside her. Gesturing around the room with her arm, she said, "And this is why I'm happy in my rental at the beach. No one bothers me there! My work's getting done, I have Sheba for company, and there are lots of nice people."

"I didn't worry about that," said her dad. "Not after talking to the Quinn guy."

She felt her jaw drop. "You what?" she asked, her voice rising.

"You think I'm going to let my only daughter go someplace I don't know about? No matter what Nonna says."

Her throat tightened. Her breathing became gasps. "And you wonder why I need to get away? Well, listen up, family. I am thirty years old, I have two college degrees, I earn my own living and don't ask for much, if anything. So stop treating me like I'm five."

"But you're alone, Kathy," said her mom quietly. "We love you very much, and we worry."

The stuffing fell out of her anger. "I love you all, too, but I'm happy the way I am. Being single is not a crime against humanity. How would you like it if I kept butting into your lives without being asked?" She twirled toward her oldest brother. "You and Jen are married for a year now. How would you like it if I asked you about having a baby? When, Joey? When are you and Jen going to have a baby? Huh?

"Well, it's not my business, so I wouldn't ask."

Her brother was silent but glanced at his wife.

"Well...now that you mention it..." said Jen shyly, caressing an almost-flat stomach.

A euphoric eruption of cheering left Kathy free to cross into the kitchen to search for her mom's cookbooks. It didn't take long before she heard footsteps.

"Can I help?" asked Marie, walking toward her daughter. "Kathy, Kathy. Come here." She wrapped her arms around her grown-up girl. "Go easy on us, honey."

Her mom was taller, and Kathy leaned in for a moment. "You should have had more daughters, Mom. Then I wouldn't be in the spotlight so often."

A slow darkness shadowed her mom's eyes, an expression Kathy had never seen before, and she shivered.

"We almost did," Marie whispered. "But...but...I lost her late in pregnancy. It was before you were born."

A vague memory stirred. Maybe she'd heard something years ago when she was a child herself? Kathy hugged her mother and rocked back and forth with her. "I'm so sorry, Mom. I don't really know about that. I'm very sorry."

"We were in a dark place, especially your dad. Thank God we had the two boys by then. A year later, when you arrived, it was like Heaven had blessed us. Daddy came back to life. So, go easy on him. On all of us. I think Joey and Nick have some memories of that time. We don't talk about it."

"No kidding," mumbled Kathy. "You guys sure know how to keep a secret." She pointed at the living room. "Hard to believe when everyone's always in each other's business."

"Eh? Doesn't mean a thing." She brushed her hands together in a way that finished the conversation. "So, why are you searching in my kitchen?"

Perfect timing for a perfect distraction, actually custom-made for her mother. "Would you like to talk about recipes with me? I need a few."

"Well, of course, sweetheart. You have some time to cook now? That's good. Don't buy instant this and instant that. All garbage. I'll make you a list." She opened a drawer and started to search.

"Mom! Just a few easy recipes."

"Better yet, come shop in my pantry. Then I'll know you have everything you need."

Suddenly, Kathy started to laugh. She laughed until her sides hurt. "Oh, Mama. You are so true to yourself."

Marie glanced at Kathy, then away. "But I'm not Nonna."

Her quiet words hit Kathy like a thunder clap. Her laughter disappeared. She looked at her mom and saw a trace of uncertainty.

"I know exactly who you are," she said, stepping closer. "You're my mom, and I love you very much."

Marie's eyes filled and she caressed her daughter's cheeks. "And I love you…and know you. And what I'm thinking is, if you're trying to cook, maybe you're not so alone at that beach…?"

CHAPTER NINE

Brandon paced up and down the driveway, Rocky at his side. "She called an hour ago. How long can it take to drive from the rotary to home? I should have followed my instincts and driven her into Beantown and picked her up. C'mon. Let's get into the car and look for her."

Just as he turned toward his vehicle, twin beams of light shone at the corner, and he spotted Kathy's Honda approaching. His body relaxed immediately, and a feeling of well-being filled him. "We've got to be thankful, Rocky. It's not late, but a human Avenger can't control icy roads."

She pulled closer toward the house, and he walked to her door. He heard Sheba from the back seat, wanting to escape.

"You want to grab her leash, Bran?" asked Kathy as she got out and stood.

"I'd much rather grab you!" he replied, putting his arms around her and leaning in with a kiss. "I was worried, Kat. You called a while ago."

"I'm sorry," she said. "I stopped off at that small grocery market outside of town. I needed a few things. You'll see when we unload."

Thirty minutes later, her small pantry was filled to the brim and her countertop hosted the overflow.

Brandon watched in amusement as she shook her head and looked totally bewildered. "How did this happen? We have enough for a siege."

"I totally agree," he said. "And what's that?" He nodded toward an old-fashioned loose-leaf notebook.

"Oh! The recipes. That's how it happened. But it's good." She looked up with dreamy eyes, came closer, and wrapped him in her arms. "I've got a lot to share with you later, when we walk on the beach."

"I'll be listening."

"It's my family," she said. "They're not as bad as I thought."

An unwanted suspicion slipped into his mind. "And what does that mean, exactly?"

"Huh?" To his relief, her confusion seemed genuine.

"Not thinking of cutting your stay here short, are you?"

Her eyes widened in shock. "No! Brandon...?" Her voice was a raspy whisper, her dark eyes shiny and her mouth, pink and waiting—for him.

He tasted her lips, lightly at first, then harder, and rejoiced at her response. "I never thought of it, not once," she added.

"I missed you, Kathy. I hope you're not planning on visiting them again for New Year's next week."

"Absolutely not. I'm staying right here—with you. Maybe your champagne will arrive by then."

"I promise you champagne," he said, "whether it arrives or not. Don't worry. We'll start the new year off with bubbles."

Her radiant smile still had the power to stop his breath. "I hope they'll be bubbles of happiness."

He didn't need champagne in order to feel happy. Being with Kat was enough. So different from other women he'd known. Kat was never boring! Smart, funny, warm…and brave. He'd never forget how she looked while insisting he save Rocky a month ago. He'd wanted a new beginning when he came to Pilgrim Cove, but he'd thought only about his career and digs. A new relationship had never been in the picture.

As he watched her talking softly to their rescues right now, his pulse raced and his heart filled with deep warmth and maybe…something more?

He'd be a fool to walk away from the possibilities.

##

Men's voices and some noise drew Kathy to her kitchen window, overlooking the backyard and the ocean. She could have easily walked out onto the deck and peeked down, but the twenty-degree temperature made her think twice. Since she'd returned from Boston a few days ago, the weather had worsened. The twice-daily walks on the beach with the dogs had become shorter.

They'd returned over an hour ago that morning, and now she was busy helping Dana solve a murder. The more she wrote, the more she discovered about her characters, the college campus, and faculty, as well as the residents of her fictional town. A third book for the series had already popped into her mind, *Murder on the Perimeter.* She liked the idea of using a math reference in each title going forward. It would set the series apart.

She'd pass the idea by Brandon. He had great marketing skills.

Her cell rang. "C'mon downstairs. I want you to meet Matt Parker. He delivered a gift to us."

"Be right there," she said with a sigh, then, patting her computer, added, "I'll be right back, Dana." Being rude was out of the question. She had to acknowledge a gift.

She donned her parka, boots, and gloves and made her way to the back of the house.

"Hey, Kathy. Look what Matt brought us." Brandon pointed at a pile of wood, stacked high. "From Bart Quinn, who, by the way, is flying back to the Sunshine State this afternoon."

"So this eases his conscience," Kathy joked as she stepped toward Matt. "Thanks for bringing it over."

"No problem," answered the tall, dark-haired man. "We all keep an eye on this house." He turned back toward Brandon. "I will warn you, however, and maybe your uncle already has, that there's no generator. If the power goes, you'll need every piece of wood in the cord, or make your way to my house, where we have a generator! Make sure you stock up on flashlights and candles."

He looked away for a moment. "I had to come rescue Laura when she stayed here. Brought her home"—he shook his head—"and we never looked back. Best thing I ever did."

Kathy smiled, a bit uncomfortable. "Good for both of you."

"Parker...Parker... Is your dad Sam Parker who meets up at the diner every morning?" asked Brandon.

Matt nodded.

"I've met him...and the rest of the bunch. My uncle brought me before I moved in. Very nice guy."

"Hey, you're preaching to the choir," said Matt with a laugh. "He lives with us. Wouldn't have it any other way." He waved and took off.

Brandon hefted a couple of wood pieces. "Open the door for me, will ya? I'll put some logs inside so we're ready."

"I enjoy a cozy fire, but do you really think we'll need them for a blackout?"

Brandon turned back toward her. "Consider me a Boy Scout. I like to be prepared"—he paused—"in all ways."

His eyes heated, and his words took on another significance. Her breath caught at the implications, and when she shivered, it wasn't because of the weather.

"Uh…Dana's waiting. I've got to get back. But I'll see you later." Whew. One hot glance from him, and she'd almost melted. Man, she had it bad. Hadn't expected…this! Whatever it was or was becoming. Two ships in the night? Or meeting the right someone?

She wasn't sixteen anymore, when she was so crazy about the new boy who'd moved in down the block, she couldn't think of anything else. Smart. Good-looking. A year older. A crush. And since then? Well, she hadn't been a nun, but no one else had made her heart race like Brandon did. No one else had made butterflies dance the tarantella inside her tummy. And no one could make her laugh as he did. All in all, a nice combination.

"Just got a call from the vet," said Brandon that evening as they prepared to take the dogs for a run. "He had good news on all fronts. His family is thriving, and two of the rescues have been adopted."

"Oh, I'm so glad," she said. "Hmm…maybe we should send them a little baby gift. We were almost witnesses!"

She felt his gaze on her and looked back. The corner of his mouth twitched. "Careful, sweetheart…getting a little involved, are we?"

"No! Anyone would say the same. And that's fabulous about the pups. I was a bit concerned since the posters were displayed only inside restaurants and supermarkets, where people could take the time to read."

"I was, too," Brandon said. "No storefronts as I'd first envisioned. But it's working. My aunt and uncle are thinking about taking one—they've had a number of dogs over the years—and if Katie Parker can ply her charms on her parents…that would make four adoptees."

"Oh, I have faith in Katie, and no doubt Sara will help to convince them. No worries there."

"Only four left, Katarina, including…"

She heard the tone in his voice. A reminder. She hadn't forgotten about the little female she'd cuddled. The adorable pup he'd omitted from his posters.

"I won't do anything that might upset Sheba," she said slowly. "So I need to call my grandmother and get her input. In any case, another visit with the little girl is in order. Maybe I was just having an emotional moment."

"Maybe," he agreed, on a totally neutral note. "You'll figure it out."

She would, but in the meantime, "C'mon. Let's run with them for two minutes." Wrapping her scarf around her mouth, she darted ahead, Sheba alongside.

Brandon passed her almost immediately and, to her surprise, leaned over and unleashed Rocky. The dog raced ahead and never looked back. Until Brandon emitted a loud whistle. Instantly, Rocky turned and ran into waiting arms. "Good boy, Rock. Good boy.

"He's panting hard and the air's cold," Brandon said. "I'm going to take him in."

"Very impressive. Have you been practicing?"

"Nope. Just thought it was time to try. I actually read the training book Adam gave me. The human has to be the alpha."

"What if he didn't come?"

"Then I would have been disappointed but not too worried. He's really smart and knows where he lives now. He would have found us."

She liked his natural use of the word *us*.

###

"Despite choosing to manage her art gallery in Florida, I think Honey regretted not going up north with Bart," said Nonna when Kathy called her on Sunday. "But she was ecstatic when he returned. And of course, I turned down their invitation to dinner last night."

That was a big mouthful for her nonna, who, as far as Kathy knew, never gossiped. "Good judgment, Nonna. She'll fly north next time. I guess Bart and Honey are—what should we call it—a second-chances couple? Very different from what you and Nonno had."

Silence on the other end, silence for a long moment. "I miss your nonno so much, Katarina. Maybe that's why I was upset with my friend. Bart and Honey are wonderful people, and they shouldn't waste time. None of us are young anymore."

Nonna was not big on sharing her deepest sensitivities, and Kathy started to be concerned. "Are you okay…?"

"Your grandpa and I had forty-five years, and it was not enough! If we'd had only twenty, I'd marry him again if he walked into my life today. Without hesitation."

Kathy heard her grandma's deep breaths through the cell. "Are you…"

"One, two, three!" Teresa continued. "We met, got engaged, and married in six months! When you know, you know."

One, two, three. Were she and Brandon on that track? "This has become a very emotional holiday season, Nonna. Maybe next year, you'll stay in Boston until afterwards. January is also a good time to fly south."

The soft chuckle reassured her. "Good idea, my brilliant granddaughter. So, how's the book coming?"

A safe subject. She brought Teresa up to date about her progress, the new website and cover design. "My downstairs neighbor is very talented with computer design. This visit is working out even better than I expected."

"You sound…happy, my Katarina. Lighthearted. Maybe a change is exactly what you needed."

"I won't argue that."

"And maybe this downstairs neighbor is also exactly what you needed. Hmm?"

Time to change the subject. "I'm thinking about adopting a rescue from the shelter run by the local vet. I'm just concerned about Sheba's reaction."

Five minutes later, she disconnected, her grandmother's last words echoing. *It's just like with your writing. If you don't try, you won't know.*

Which held true about anything in life. The women in her family seemed to put the challenge into practice. Between Nonna's passionate revelations about her wonderful marriage and her mom's revelations of a painful time, she'd learned more about her family than she would have guessed lay hidden behind an invisible Russo curtain.

##

"Only four dogs left, but Brandon told me to hold this little girl for you," said Adam as he led Kathy and Sheba to the kennels.

"He's thoughtful that way." And smart, convincing her that either decision she made would be correct.

"There's no right or wrong about this," Brandon had said when she'd left the house. "It either works or it doesn't. You'll know." Then he wished her luck and went back inside, his mind clearly elsewhere.

"Okay, Sheba. You're going to help me out here. You have a big say in this."

Thirty minutes later, Kathy laughed at herself while she cuddled the newest member of the family. "I can't believe that she remembers me," she said to Adam. "At least, she acts that way."

"Her scent memory is excellent, as in most dogs, but you held her for a long time when she was not in a good place. At heart, dogs are pack animals, which is why Sheba's so good with this. She's got a playmate."

"She'll have two playmates for a while. Good grief, Adam. You might say that Sea View House has gone to the dogs."

His eyes twinkled. "But, thanks to you, this rescue is *embarking* on a new journey."

Oh, she loved puns. Her mind raced. "I'm not even *pawsing* for another minute to think it *rover*. Thanks *furry* much."

"Oh, my God, Dad. She's as bad as you are." Sara headed straight to Kathy. "Are you adopting her?"

"I am."

The girl's grin crossed her face. "Then she'll have a wonderful home." She crouched next to Sheba, who nuzzled into the child. "And you're going to be the best big sister ever. Just like me."

The love she saw in Adam's eyes when he looked at his daughter... Kathy felt her own eyes fill and blinked hard. Time to change the subject. "Hey, Sara. We need a name. Got any ideas?" She wasn't expecting a bull's-eye response, just wanted to make conversation.

"Let me think a minute." Sara looked between Sheba and the rescue a few times. "We've got the Queen of Sheba, so maybe we should call her Cleopatra. Cleo. Two queens."

"Cleo," repeated Kathy. "Short, definite clear sound. I like it." She looked down at the pup. "Do you feel like a Cleo?"

She received a lick and a kiss.
"Then Cleo it is!" She glanced at Adam, whose eyes still followed his daughter.

"Hey, Adam. If Sara ever wants coaching in advanced mathematics—you know, they stuff they don't do in regular school—call me. No charge."

He nodded. "I thought you were a writer."

"I am. By way of math and statistics. It's a long story."

He chuckled. "Welcome to Pilgrim Cove. Everyone has a story. You fit right in."

"Not quite there yet," she said, leashing Cleo. "Who knows?"

"Took me some time, too. I wasn't born here. Neither was Becca, but circumstances..." He shrugged.

"One of my circumstances is back at the house. He's playing it cool, but I bet he's curious."

Adam grinned. "Oh, I know he is."

"Well, thanks *furry* much," she said with a wink.

"*Ap-paws, ap-paws.* Thanks to you and Brandon, we're down to three healthy canines left to give away. Besides two newly arrived greyhounds." He sighed. "Wonderful dogs. I wish all those racetracks would close."

Kathy had never thought about that world and could only imagine.

Sara helped getting the supplies to the car while Kathy held both leashes. She watched Sheba step in front, turn her head, woof-talk to Cleo. No confusion about who was in charge. "Atta girl, Sheba. Keep her in line, because I still need a peaceful place to get work done."

##

As soon as she pulled into the driveway, Brandon came out his front door onto the porch, jogged down the steps, and greeted her with a kiss. "You've got your hands full. Happy?" He leaned down to pet both dogs.

She nodded. "I think it's the right decision. She's a sweetheart. And Sheba's so good with her."

"I'll bring the food and bowls and whatever else you decided to load up on while you go on upstairs with them. Show the pup her new home."

"Okay and thanks." She looked at the dogs and said, "Home." Sheba went toward the back of the house and Cleo followed. Two smarties.

They clambered upstairs to the landing, where Kathy came to a complete stop. On the door was a large colorful poster. It read:

Welcome home, Cleo.
This is the only pup tent you'll ever need.

An enlarged photo of the dog sat below the printed words. A sprinkle of hearts surrounded the pup. Hearts that matched the ones from the Avenger illustrations Brandon had drawn of her.

She studied the poster again, absorbing the message. And that's when she started to cry. No mystery here. Rather, a love story, illuminated with words and pictures.

Footsteps sounded behind her. She turned around and walked right into his waiting arms. "Bran...?" She snuggled closer and didn't want to be anywhere else.

"Yeah...I-I guess I communicated."

"And I guess you got Adam to communicate, too."

"Guilty. He didn't mind at all!"

Laughter chased her tears, and she took note of the surroundings. So much life, so much love. "C'mon, I'll fix dinner."

"Good. I'm starving."

"You're always starving, and you're not one of those starving-artist types."

"I'd better not be," he said. "You can't build a future on air."

CHAPTER TEN

After taking the dogs to the curb midmorning for an extra outing, Kathy knocked on the downstairs door and walked into Brandon's kitchen with her four-legged charges. He was leaning against the table, phone to his ear. He glanced up, smiled, and finished the call.

"Reminding Cleo of her responsibilities?" he asked.

Kathy chuckled. "Something like that. I think I made a good decision. Cleo's been really good, happy to sleep near Sheba, and is settling in well."

"Of course she's happy next to Sheba because they're both in the same room with you." He held up his hand in a stop motion. "It's not a criticism. Rocky sleeps in my room, too. Don't you, boy?" He leaned over to scratch the dog behind the ears and received a lick of thanks.

"You're awfully good with him," said Kathy, "especially when you didn't want him in the first place."

Brandon cupped his hands over Rocky's ears. "Don't let him hear you!"

The man was funny. He made her laugh a lot. "Ever think about stand-up? I bet you'd get a following."

He eye-rolled her but said, "As long as you're amused, I'm happy. Unfortunately, you may not want to hear this next news."

"What?" He seemed so serious, she held her breath.

"I was too late in making dinner reservations for tonight at the Wayside Inn. It's New Year's Eve, and I wanted to take you out for a change. They have live music. I'm sorry."

He really did look rueful. Silly man. "Are you already tired of my cooking?" she teased.

"No chance," he said, perking up. "It's not as bad as I expected. I think you actually surprised yourself." He walked toward her and gave her a quick kiss. "I'm not tired of anything yet and don't expect to be."

His compliment made her blush, and she felt heat rise to her face. "I'm not really disappointed about going out," she said. "It's kind of soon to leave Cleo alone for an evening anyway, don't you think?"

He glanced at the dogs. "Not alone. I trust Sheba. But I have another idea. We can celebrate with the champagne that just arrived."

The best-selling author had come through. Didn't forget the "little" people. She tucked the knowledge away. Maybe someday… "Very nice. A liquid dinner, huh?"

"Okay, you've got a point. Give me a sec, and I'll come up with something." His fingers tapped on the table. His brows furrowed and cleared almost immediately. "Let's call the Lobster Pot and get a few lobsters to go."

"Oh, I like that idea." An intimate dinner at home. "Life is so strange—and funny, too. Who knew six weeks ago, we'd each be involved in a new relationship on New Year's Eve? I wasn't looking for one, and you…? I don't think so, either."

A crooked smile crossed his face, and he nodded. "Totally correct. Women were last on my list when I came here." His eyes shone with laughter. "So, later on, when folks ask us how we met, we can truthfully say we met by accident. A fortunate accident."

Later on. He was talking about a future. She stepped closer toward him, looked into his eyes, and that was all the encouragement he needed.

"So beautiful," he murmured before his mouth touched hers with a slow, thoughtful kiss, which sent a tingle down her body. She embraced him and could feel muscles ripple along his back beneath his sweater. She pressed her hands against them, traveling higher and lower, wanting to discover more of him. His tongue traced the edges of her mouth, and she shivered again, parting her lips just enough to taste him.

When he stepped back, she felt adrift and almost moaned. He smiled. "That was the appetizer."

She was ready for the meal.

##

The wind had whipped up, and clouds covered the sky. Neither moon nor stars could be seen. Brandon shut the engine of his SUV and jogged into the restaurant. Maybe it was fortunate he and Kathy were staying in that night. Living at the beach, in a beach town had made him more aware of weather than he'd been in Boston, where a landlord was responsible for shoveling the sidewalk and fixing whatever broke. In Sea View House, it was up to him and Kathy and a group of retirees. His cell rang and he looked down. Speaking of...

"Hey, Uncle Ralph, just thinking of you and your cronies." He held on and shook his head once or twice while his uncle spoke.

"A nor'easter, you say? I did buy several flashlights and batteries, but I hadn't really been checking the forecast." He should have been, and listened again while Ralph brought him up to date. Until finally, "Yep, I'll keep an eye on Kathy. Don't you worry about that! You stay safe, too. Love to Aunt Linda."

Chuckling, he hung up. His uncle wasn't stupid. He'd found out what he really wanted to know about the Sea View House residents. Brandon, however, now had more concerns about the potential storm. He'd lived through enough nor'easters to know they were serious business and could be unrelenting for several days. He started making a mental list of what to check on when he returned home.

He noticed his rescue poster still in the waiting area and waved to Maggie Sullivan, who was visiting from table to table, presiding over an almost full house. A mid-week New Year's Eve at the Lobster Pot seemed as busy as a regular Saturday night. *Good for you all.* He appreciated the hard work of a family business where it was front and center to the owners twenty-four seven. Very similar to his business, except for one major item. When it came to making decisions, every decision was his own. He threw back his shoulders and stretched. It had worked so far—in fact, he was finally loaded with work once again. He hadn't lost talent, skills, or a good list of clients. He'd lost time.

Hmm...and now he had to make time for Kathy's new website. The design would require an in-depth interview so he could understand the image she wanted to convey. He also wanted to redesign the cover of her first book to create a brand that carried over to the second one. Ideas kept coming, and it wasn't until he paid for the dinner and stepped into the ice-cold wind, which hit him in the face, that he was recalled to practical matters—a defensive game plan for Sea View House.

##

"A traditional division of labor," Kat said, standing in front of the sink in Brandon's apartment, tossing a salad. "I'm in the kitchen, and you're gathering wood. We could be cave people."

"Whatever works is good for me," he replied, hefting several logs and kindling in his arms as he walked down the center hall toward the living room near the front of the house. Despite the threat of weather, he whistled as he arranged the wood. A fire set the stage for romance. Right?

Hold that thought, fella. In the end, he was New England born and bred and went to check on supplies. Extra blankets? Yes, on the top shelves of each bedroom closet. Something he hadn't noticed before. He gathered them up and brought them to the living room.

"Have you got any matches hiding in these drawers?" he asked on his way back through the kitchen to get more wood.

"Don't you have enough logs yet?" asked Kathy when he returned with the next load. She held up an old-fashioned box of wooden matches for him to see.

"All depends."

Her brow rose in question.

"A cozy evening or a freezing night? Or a freezing three days? You never know with this kind of storm."

"Oh, my...right...if the electricity goes, or rather *when* it goes." She frowned and bit her lip. "Yeah, you'd better bring in more. And I'll put on my jacket and help you pile some logs right outside the kitchen door."

"Thanks, but I can handle that. How about feeding the hounds now? An earlier schedule for walking them."

"Good idea."

"And one more thing—how much food do we have between us? Enough for at least three days?"

"Are you kidding? I can feed us for a week or more—as long as you like hot dogs toasted in the fire." He gave her a thumbs-up and left.

By the time he came in with the next load of logs, the dogs were happily munching, each with an individual bowl. He paused on his way back out, just inhaling the sight of his own kitchen, inhaling the sight of a busy Katarina in a bright red turtleneck sweater, with her dark wavy hair scrunched behind her neck. Focused. Always involved, always trying to make things better.

"Hey," he said softly.

She glanced up immediately.

"We're a good team."

He didn't need an outside storm. Her smile had the power of an electric jolt. And it got him every time.

##

The kitchen would have to do. She wasn't going to disturb the potpourri of Brandon's work and materials covering the large dining room table. She found a tablecloth in the linen closet and spread it out. Plates, silverware... She searched for champagne glasses and settled for wine goblets. She'd bought some frozen spanakopita for an appetizer. Salad was done; lobster waited in the fridge for rewarming. She'd throw a couple of potatoes in the microwave. Everything was in order.

"I'll be back in a few," she called to Brandon.

"Back? Where're you going?" he asked, meeting her in the hallway, crumpled newspaper in his hand.

"My place. I want to clean up a bit." She batted her lashes. "After all, it's our second real date."

His gaze swept over her, returning to her face. "You look beautiful," he said quietly. "No need to go outside."

Her hair was a mess, and she'd worn the same clothes all day…but the way he looked at her, the way he devoured her…he'd spoken the truth. His truth.

"I guess it really is in the eye of the beholder," she whispered, admiring his broad shoulders and pecs outlined in his navy-blue thermal tee shirt. She could smell the cold air that clung to him from his forays outside.

His gaze darkened, then softened. His arms came around her, and his lips caressed hers. Like a match to kindle, she burst into flame. Intense desire raced through her, so unexpected at that moment, but so delicious. She shivered.

He felt her reaction. She knew he did. Tilting his head back, he questioned her with his eyes.

She raised to her tiptoes, kissed him, and whispered, "Forget the lobster. I'm ready for dessert."

"It's about time!" he replied. "I've been ready since we met."

An honorable man. How lucky could a gal get?

##

"We both must have been more than ready," Brandon said with a rueful laugh thirty minutes later.

Kathy rolled on her side, one arm across his chest, her fingers interlacing with the wiry hair she found. "I won't argue that."

"Good, because you'd be lying if you did."

"I'd also be lying if I said that this"—she gestured across the bed, encompassing them both—"meant nothing. It's been quite a while…" Her voice trailed off.

His finger gently closed her lips. "It means more than you can know. You're so different, so real."

"Oh, I'm real, all right. In my family, you can't dream your life away. Feet are definitely on the ground. Maybe you hung around the wrong clubs, with the wrong people, and now you're wising up."

He tucked her against his shoulder. "You could be right, but maybe it's this place."

"The magic stuff?"

One brow lifted. "I won't go that far, but staying here gets you off the old treadmill. Shakes up your life."

"How quickly they forget," she quoted airily. "Brandon, your life was already topsy-turvy by being evicted and having to rebuild your business."

He flipped his hand at those remarks. "Fixable. Both situations. My life was rocked from the foundation as soon as I met my unexpected housemate. Every day since then has been an adventure."

She bestowed a line of kisses along his jaw. "Have I rattled your life, Brandon?"

"Come here, and don't ask silly questions."

"I'm already here," she whispered—just as her stomach growled.

She couldn't have decided who laughed harder, but just then, the dogs began to howl outside the bedroom door. And the laughter began again.

"Like I said before," Brandon offered, getting out of bed, "it's never boring around here."

"It's just...life," Kathy said. For the first time, she wondered if that's the way her own mom viewed their family gatherings. Not a crowd of disparate people creating chaos but the embodiment of family enjoying one another. Enjoying life.

They leashed the dogs, stepped outside the front door, where Kathy was blown three steps back by the wind. "I hope they all take care of business now," she said, feeling for the plastic bags in her pocket. "I sure don't want to come out again in an hour. This mist is turning into icy needles."

"Not a problem," said Brandon, nodding at the canines. "They don't like it out here, either. They're almost good to go back."

She produced the plastic bags and gave one to Brandon. "The first year I took Sheba for the winter, I never even thought about the details of dog sitting. Welcome to the club."

"No problem. Rocky's a keeper, and I'm still amazed I took him in."

And she was amazed he hadn't realized what a loving heart beat in his chest. "I've got to go upstairs and get some clothes, Brandon. I really do."

"We'll both go," he said, "after we put the dogs inside my place. C'mon, they're ready."

They started walking up the driveway, the pooches leading the way. "I'm perfectly capable..." Kathy began when Brand interrupted.

"I know you are, but I want to check the windows and slightly turn the spigots in the sinks. Prevents freezing."

"The ROMEOs will be happy to save on a nasty bill. How do you know these things?" asked Kathy.

He opened the back door, let the dogs into his place, and they both headed upstairs.

"I come from a family in the building trades. Ralph's the electrician. My dad's a plumber, carpenter, general contractor… He can do anything that needs doing."

"Wow. Did you trail around after him when you were little, like a father-son duet?"

He shook his head. "When I was a kid, he worked for other people, and kids didn't hang around. Liability stuff."

She nodded. "Right. It's called risk. I calculate those things."

"I know. So now I'm wondering…do you include relationship risks in your data?"

Shocked at the question, she twirled to see him better and relaxed. His grin and gleaming eyes said everything. She tossed her head. "Personal relationships are incalculable. It's a risk you have to take."

An hour later, Brandon wondered if he could risk standing up without embarrassing himself. Did Kat have any idea how sensuous she made the art of eating a lobster? Her lips glistened after she dipped each morsel of meat in butter and brought it to her mouth. Her tongue peeked out to taste before she savored each piece, chewing slowly as though it were her last meal on earth. He glanced at his own plate. Only a claw remained, and he couldn't remember eating the rest.

"Oh, this is delicious," she said while tearing off one of the antennae that he'd ignored. He watched her lips purse around it as she nibbled the meat from one end, broke it, and worked the other end.

"Geez, Kat, there's nothing in those spikes. What are you doing besides driving me nuts?"

Her eyes half closed. "I guess I didn't tell you that lobster was my very favorite treat. Even better than steak, and I absolutely l-o-v-e steak."

Steak had to be easier than this.

"And I guess I never mentioned that it takes me an hour to get through one lobster. I waste nothing in these babies."

He glanced at the third innocent crustacean waiting for them and groaned. She'd be at the table forever at this rate. He sat back in his chair. Might as well enjoy the show.

Two more antennae and then the second claw. Butter, lips, tongue…oh, jeez Louise, this was tough.

She tilted her head and leaned forward. "Didn't you like your food, Bran? I followed the warming directions exactly—wrapped them in heavy foil with butter, low oven for no more than ten minutes. Do you want to trade? Mine tastes really good."

"My plate's empty." His voice sounded gravelly, even to him.

"But did you enjoy it? You're so…quiet."

"Loved every bite, but you take your time, Kat." He nodded toward the serving dish where the extra lobster waited. "I'll be right back." He went to the dining room, grabbed some markers, colored pencils, and paper, and returned. In moments, he lost track of time while a rendering of *Kat and Her Prey* took shape. Full face, chin up, lips shiny, a forkful of lobster meat approaching her mouth. Her eyes shone back at him.

The room was quiet except for Kathy's occasional sighs of contentment. And her complaints thrown in from time to time. "I hope you know what you're doing. I'd better like it, but if it's a caricature, it'll be fine. No more Avenger girl, though. Those days are over."

"Stop worrying and enjoy the poor lobster. I'm surprised you didn't move to Maine and fish for them yourself."

"Very funny. I drive my brothers crazy, too. They hate eating seafood with me. Maybe it's a man thing."

And maybe she was nervous about his sketch. She eyed the extra lobster. "Let's save it for tomorrow. I can chop it with celery and make salad for sandwiches."

A wonderful reprieve for his libido. "Great idea! You wrap it and I'll clear the rest away."

She grabbed a napkin, wiped her hands, and walked over to him. "Not until I see what you've done this time."

He positioned the picture in her line of vision and watched her absorb it. Not a caricature, not a cartoon or superhero style. Simply the real Katarina.

To his horror, her mouth trembled, and her eyes filled with tears. "It's not fair," she whispered. "You could see what I feel, and it wasn't about the lobster. I was staring at you the whole time, and it's right there! On the page."

He took another look at what he'd rendered. Good lord, she was right. She'd revealed herself, and he'd captured it. Her truth.

Standing up, he put the picture aside and wrapped her in his arms. "But it's all good, Kat. Because I feel the same."

CHAPTER ELEVEN

A unique awareness permeated the air as they cleaned the kitchen. A tingling that bordered on electric. Whenever their hands touched, Kathy glanced up and received a quick kiss. She couldn't stop smiling. Like lightning in her blood, she was alive to his presence. Was this what love felt like? If she could carry a tune, she'd sing. The only music she heard now, however, was nature at its most raw. The wind moaned and whipped around the house, stronger with each gust and—she listened harder...

"Brandon? I hear the ocean. It's roaring. Something's happening out there." She ran to the back window.

"High surf probably." He joined her, the dogs at his heels. "It's pitch-black. I can't see anything at all, can you?"

"Nope, not even our own porch right outside this window." She stroked his arm. "I've been through many storms, blizzards, and hurricanes. All in town. I've never witnessed a nor'easter right on the ocean, at the coastline. Oh, my."

"Don't worry, Kat. This house is solid, and you're not alone." He wrapped his arms around her. "We'll be fine. But I have a notion the beach won't look the same afterwards. Those heavy waves we're hearing are going to affect this coastline and cause some erosion."

The lights flickered, and she startled. His arms tightened around her. "I'm not scared. This is just…eerie."

"Good word. Did you ever think of writing?"

She chuckled, and he loosened his hold. "But let's take that flickering light as a warning," Brandon said, reaching for the matches. "It's time to build the fire. I waited as long as possible to preserve supplies, but waiting's no longer an option." He walked toward the living room and Rocky followed immediately. Sheba and Cleo looked from her to Brandon.

Kathy waved her arm. "Go ahead, girls, I'll be right there." And off they went.

She did a last check of the kitchen, found some plastic cups, and took the open champagne bottle with her. *I feel bubbly and happy even without the champagne.*

"Wow. You've got enough blankets to keep Alaska warm."

"It might feel like Alaska if the power blows. Hopefully, this baby will keep us from freezing."

The kindling had caught, and Brandon was feeding it with a couple of smaller logs to get a true fire blazing. A lock of dark hair curled over his forehead while capable hands manipulated the materials.

Kathy reached for her phone. "Look at me, Bran." *Click. Click.*

"Is turnabout fair play?" he asked with a wink.

"You have no competition from me. I'm hoping they come out halfway decently." She checked the phone for the result. "Halfway it is," she reported with a sigh.

"You know what they say about practice?"

She threw a mock glare at him. "Are you kidding? I've got enough on my plate. You're the artist in this house. And that's final!"

He approached with a wicked grin. "Then let's practice something else. We had our dessert earlier. Are you ready for the main event?"

She melted under his gaze. Her heart was his. "We're probably the only ones in town who think this coziness is romantic." She held out her hand, and he tucked it in his larger one. She felt a kiss on her temple.

"Except for the howling wind, pelting sleet and icy snow…and those flickering lights...then yeah. It's romantic enough for me."

With that short warning, the house went dark. "Timing, as they say, is everything," said Brandon. "Hold on to the romantic thought while I work on the fire. It's too soon to ignore it for long. It might go out."

"Well, at least dinner is behind us," said Kathy, making her way to the sofa.

"The only hot food we'll have from now on is what we can toast in here," he said while adding another log. "But we've got storm windows and great insulation. The ROMEOs do a great job with this place."

"They answer to that William Adams Foundation, and they're keeping insurance rates down," said Kathy. "They really have no choice."

"There are always choices," he said.

"Maybe for some, but not when Bart Quinn is chairman of the board."

Brandon threw back his head and laughed heartily. "It's probably a position for life!" He stood and examined the room. "I'll get a couple of flashlights. Then we'll move the couch closer to the fireplace…"

"You've got it all figured out, huh?"

He was quiet for a moment. "All? No, just some of it. Storm prep is pretty simple. People are more complicated."

Her stomach tightened. "How about the people in this room?"

He walked toward her, lifted her chin, and bestowed a kiss that ran deep. "Of course we're complicated. We're human. But I'd say it works for us."

"And I agree." But their tucked-away Wonderland life had to end soon, and then a new reality would lie ahead. As she thought back, she realized the *L* word hadn't come up in conversation. She'd seen his admiration of her reflected in his drawings and pictures. She'd certainly felt it in his touch and embrace. Evidence was everywhere! But as delightful as that was, she wanted to hear the one word too important to be forced. The one word, she realized, that neither of them had uttered aloud.

##

In the glow of the firelight, Kathy watched Brandon stoke the flames. His dark hair shone with hints of red as he worked, his hands adept with his chore and his profile etched in concentration. His navy thermal tee pulled tautly across his back, revealing a pair of broad shoulders. The longer she watched him, the harder she tried to tamp down the racing current inside her. Never before had she been so attracted to any man. Never before had she worked to hold back a moan.

He stood, replaced the fire screen, and approached. One look at her and his eyes blazed. "You are not alone, Katarina."

And then she wasn't. He climbed in beside her, adjusting to the narrow seat, and lowered his head until his mouth touched hers. She pulled him closer, totally absorbed in the kiss, and followed him down to the carpeted floor, on top of the blankets and pillows he'd gathered earlier. Good idea.

"You're a beautiful woman, Kat, inside and out." His kiss trailed down her neck and stopped at her shirt. "Do you need this?"

"You're supplying enough heat," she whispered, pulling off the garment. "But two is only fair." She tugged at his tee, and in a moment, her hands explored the hardness of his chest, her fingers weaving through the coarse hair, pausing on his nipples, teasing them.

"Oh, nice," he gasped. He rolled on his side, his hand caressing her bare stomach before his fingers slowly trailed up the center of her chest, pausing a moment at the clasp of her bra before freeing her. They continued around one breast, then around the other, slowly, deftly. And again.

Her breath caught with sharp gasps of excitement each time his hand circled closer to his goal, toward each peak, closer and closer. He leaned over and gently blew across her nipples. Her entire body tightened, and she clutched the blanket at her side as her moans escaped. His tongue found one nub and his fingers found the other. Her head rolled from side to side.

"Ooh…"

"I love seeing you like this," he whispered.

She reached for his waistband. "I want you with me."

"Wonderful idea." He tugged his pants off in one quick motion, and she drew him down toward her. "Hang on a sec," he said, "and I'll love you all night."

She heard a ripping sound. "Smart," she whispered, reaching to embrace him, vaguely remembering his earlier use of the protection.

"Now where was I?" His tongue found its target again, and she felt her breast swell under his touch. God, her nipples were so sensitive. His slow hand made its way down to her thighs, to that corner where they met, where her pleasure point was the greatest. Shivers rippled through her.

"Brandon, come to me," she gasped.

"Not yet..." He kissed every inch of her from neck to waist, and as she quivered and moaned, he slowly lowered himself, slowly inched himself through the narrow opening, to that private place she wanted to share. She grasped him around the waist and pulled him closer. "Come on. It's okay."

But still he paused. "Shh...want to make sure..."

She tightened around him, knowing he couldn't hold back another moment--which he didn't. And she welcomed him inside.

Brandon knew he held an unexpected gift in his arms, a gift he had not sought but found. Katarina. A delightful, loving, wonderful prize, and he hadn't wanted to spoil it. He'd tried to enter her carefully, but she was ready for him and the ride began. They found their tempo quickly, her eyes glowing from within. The happier she was, the happier he became. At times, their bodies moved in such exquisite harmony, he didn't know where he left off and she began. As if they were one. She was so different from any other woman he'd known. He explored every inch of her, but she did the same with him. Their kisses led everywhere.

They rode the waves, sharing the discovery of new lovers, knowing that they were special in the universe. Surely, they were. And after the exquisite explosion, after the fireworks had cooled, she nestled against him, her head on his chest near his shoulder as naturally as if she'd been there a million times. He picked up a dark curl and held it gently.

"I can't fall asleep before I rebuild the fire," he said quietly.

"Uber man—you get an A in the 'building fires' department."

"You imp!" He waited a bit, as new ideas accosted him and filled his mind. "Kat? Hmm…I'm thinking…you know…about us."

He heard her inhale. "I'm definitely listening."

"We're good together, aren't we? Happy, too."

Her short pause seemed like years. "Yes, I think we are. And not only"—she waved at the linen—"in here."

Bingo! She'd hit it. That was the difference from his relationship with Amber. With Kat he felt joy and pleasure in the small things as well as the large. They shared ideas, supported and helped one another. Any stress they'd faced flew in from the outside. Sure, the physical attraction might have come first, but alone, it would not be enough to sustain a full life. He knew that now. He also knew that he wanted that full life and all the chaos that went with it. Heaven on earth would be sharing that life with Katarina Russo.

He rolled on his side, leaned down, and kissed her again. "I've never been happier, Katarina. I love you. Simply put, there's no one else in this world for me."

Tears rolled down her cheeks, and his heart almost stopped until he remembered that women and men were different. "I hope those are happy tears?"

"Bingo."

##

Snow still fell steadily the next morning when Kathy and Brandon walked the dogs in front of the house.

"As if the snow isn't enough, it's almost eight and it's pitch-black out here. Just like inside. What is wrong with this picture? We should be visiting Nonna in Florida!"

"Some of us have to work for a living," said Brandon, "including you. Be careful where you walk. In these cold temperatures, sleet freezes to ice on the ground. If it happens over and over, like it's done this winter, it can turn into a thick base coat of black ice."

"Dangerous stuff. I know all about it. Which is why I like taking the T instead of driving this time of year."

She meant the MTA—Boston trains. Okay. He'd be flexible about places. "So you're thinking Boston is the better idea?'"

She stopped in her tracks, shaking her head. "Actually, I wasn't thinking at all. Just reacting to what you said about black ice."

"Not to worry, Kat," he said with a laugh. "You have a built-in Uber guy." She stared right at him, and even through the falling snow, he could see her wide smile.

"So I do. I really did pick a winner," she said, giving his arm a squeeze. "Although I had to convince you to adopt Rocky."

"I did better than you," he countered. "I picked two winners!"

"And don't forget it!" Kathy said. "Oh, Bran, isn't this fun?"

He knew what she meant. The nonsense, the discovery, the going to the next level. The novelty for all those who'd found love for the first time.

"The best of fun. This storm, however, is no longer fun. Any chance you can conjure up something for breakfast? I worked up an appetite last night."

"Really? I wouldn't have believed it if I weren't there myself."

He stepped closer, keeping the leashes apart, and put his arm around her. "A perfect night." Her cheeks turned red, and he knew it was not from the cold.

"Hard boiled eggs, PBJs, or cold cereal with milk," she offered. "All safe. I put the milk outside last night."

Laughing, he said, "Is that your way of changing the subject?"

"It's…it's all so new," she said quietly.

Brandon kept his arm around her as they made their way up the driveway and back into his kitchen. "I need to bring more wood inside so our good fire doesn't go out."

"I can help," she said, crouching to wipe the dogs dry and clean their feet. "We don't know how long this outage will last."

His cell phone rang. "Hey, Uncle Ralph. What's the word?" He held up a finger to Kat. "Yeah, yeah. A few more hours. Okay. By tonight at the latest. Take care. Thanks."

"That's not too bad," said Kathy. "At least we can count on a hot dinner."

And that's what he loved about her. Lemons to lemonade. He leaned down and kissed her—just because he wanted to. Her happy smile filled him with well-being. "Love you for that."

"I don't ever guarantee what I'll actually produce… You know me by now."

"Wasn't referring to the food, just to you seeing the sunny side."

She winked at him. "It's a newly acquired skill. That visit with my family made a difference."

Her family. From what he'd picked up, there'd be a lot of noise, opinions, and personalities. He stood a bit taller and stretched his shoulders back.

"Invite them down, Kat. I'd like to meet them, and I don't want to remain a mystery man." He'd handle whomever and whatever he had to.

"Not yet," she said. "I'm not quite down the finish line. And endings have to be…just so."

"You've lost me," he said, ready to go out again. "Don't you want me to meet them?"

"Of course. But you know my deadline is Valentine's Day." She began pacing. "Only six weeks! Not one person except Nonna respects my writing time. If I invite them next week, I'll be inundated by calls every day thereafter and get nothing done." She stopped walking and shook her head. "Nope. Maybe in February. We'll see."

He got it. Finishing her book was the whole reason she was in Pilgrim Cove in the first place. "Totally your call. Whatever works for you, I'm on board. What a coincidence that we both make our living on deadlines."

She held her hand up like a traffic cop. "I can hardly call my writing *making a living* but maybe one day… I just hope I'm not fooling myself," she said quietly. "So much competition, so many doubts. And then, there's my other career, which I also love."

"Having choices is great." He knew little about her insurance job, but thought her first book was pretty good. "Don't think about the competition. Just focus on the manuscript. If I worried about every other graphic artist out there, I'd never get out of bed in the morning."

"But you're so good!" she said, standing still and looking amazed.

"Everyone has doubts. I hate to say it, kiddo, but you're not as unique as you think—except, of course, to me." He embraced her. Kissed her. And vowed to start on her website. That should perk her up. And he'd straighten out her family, too.

CHAPTER TWELVE

If she didn't stop daydreaming, nothing would get done! A week after the New Year's Eve storm, Kathy sat at her computer, humming under her breath while she worked numbers to help a new client company establish a first-ever retirement plan. The company had grown since opening two years before, and she needed to determine what they could afford to offer employees without incurring risk to themselves. After that, she'd continue with the family risk project—why some people wanted to engage in rock climbing while having small children, she didn't understand. But she didn't have to. If she ever had a child, rock climbing was out! But skiing…well, that was another matter.

Oh, for crying out loud, Kathy. Focus!

Her phone dinged and she looked at the text. *Are we ready for dinner?*

Lost track of time. Come on up.

She glanced at the wall clock, stood quickly, and stretched. Laughing ruefully at her stiffness, she planned on a long walk with the dogs that evening.

She heard her door open and then the kitchen was filled with man. A man who swooped in for a kiss. "How was your day, my little Kat?"

"So good that I need some exercise later. Let's do the beach tonight." She walked toward the pantry, then opened the fridge. "Leftovers okay?"

"Since when am I fussy?"

Smiling inside, she brought out a bowl of meatballs and transferred the food to a pot for a stovetop reheat. "That's one of the things I love about you," she said. "You're easy!"

"Insulting my virtue, huh?" His eyes gleamed as he stole another kiss. "I want to show you something after dinner." He hefted his laptop and placed it near hers at the end of the long table.

"New project?"

"You could say that."

She boiled some pasta while he filled the dog bowls, pausing to pet Sheba and Cleo, who'd greeted him as if they hadn't seen him in years.

"And you're my boy, Rocky," he continued, "You get the credit—for all this."

Amused and content, Kathy continued to assemble the meal. "Set the table, will you?"

He opened the correct closet door with the familiarity of one who knew his way around. Then he sniffed the air. "Smells good in here. I don't know why you downplay your skills. We haven't had a bad meal yet, not even once!"

"That's because, at the very least, I'm better than you. Between the two of us, we won't starve, but just wait until you taste my mother's cooking. You'll see the difference."

"I've already had your mom's food. Way back when you brought a carton back from Boston. It was great, but so is yours."

She walked to him and cupped his cheek. "Is that what's meant by *love is blind?*"

He shrugged, but a smile tugged at the corner of his mouth. "Just telling the truth."

"I'm glad you're happy, but cooking is not my priority, never has been." She focused her gaze down the table toward her computer. "Everything that's important to me, that's part of me and who I am, is in that laptop." She pointed at it and looked up at him. "Our careers say a lot about us."

His brow rose in curiosity. "That's true, but it isn't the complete picture."

"Well, of course not. We're about people and love and family, too. But we spend an awful lot of time working. I'm a firm believer in not waking up with a bellyache every morning!"

"No argument here," he said, grinning. "Who wants to live that way?"

"But people do, Bran. That's the awful thing. Many people do dread going to work."

He shrugged and said, "In the end, it comes down to opportunity and choices. I think people usually figure out how to make their lives work."

She stabbed a fork through a piece of penne and held it up. "Let's see what happens…" She raised her arm.

"What are you do—"

She threw the pasta against the wall. It stuck, and she grinned at him. "I've always wanted to try that."

"Like your mom?" he asked, shaking his head with amusement.

"Are you kidding? Her pasta always comes out perfectly, but from now on I'll use the wall method."

Suddenly she was in his arms, held tightly, and being danced around the room. "You, Katarina, are my perfect pasta. No wall involved."

She snuggled closer. "You were right," she said. "People usually figure out how to make things work."

##

As they cleared up a while later, Brandon's thoughts raced to the ideas he'd brought to show Kat. Surprisingly, a bit of anxiety flowed through him. Almost as though she were a paying client he had to please.

"C'mon," he said, reaching for his laptop. "I want to show you a few concepts I came up with."

She tilted her head and blinked once or twice. "What kind?"

Did she not have a clue? He'd promised her a redesign for her internet presence. "Sit down and you'll see."

He opened the computer and pulled up a file labeled *Kat-Bk. Covers*.

"Let's talk about your book covers first, which means font, logo, color, mood—an attractive picture that will make the book fly off the shelves—so to speak. Let's say, fly into someone's e-reader."

"Okay..." she drew out the word. "I'm listening."

He shifted slightly to study her. Blank expression except for a narrow line in her forehead. "So, would I be correct in thinking you're clueless?"

She leaned back, her body stiffening, and then she giggled. "Why should I deny it? The way I see it, my job is to write the book—not a small thing—and pay someone to do what I can't."

"Fair enough, but now sit up and learn. I need your input if we're to come up with your brand. Luckily, I ignored the cover and actually read your first book, so I've got some ideas. You're my client now, and I want you to be happy."

That fabulous smile lit up her face, and Brandon knew he'd sit there all night, if necessary, in order to keep seeing it. As he spoke, however, Kat got more excited. A logo hinting of a college campus with Dana Moretti in profile. Or facing out. He showed her both. *A Foul Day on Campus* across the top with the series name across the bottom: *A Dana Moretti Mystery, Book 1*. With a touch of a key, he flipped their positions.

"Lots of choices," Kat said. "I like that. And I like where you placed my name, and the font size. Readers will see it."

"That's the idea," he said. "I put Dana in a red sweater. Red stands out. Readers will recognize her soon, and know that this is the series they want."

"Right. Good idea." Her face scrunched up. "I kind of look good in red myself."

Her inflection carried such surprise and innocence, he couldn't stop laughing. "I know, Ms. Alter Ego Moretti."

"Oh, you're right. I forgot about that for a moment." She tapped her fingers over her mouth. "But you know what? I think Dana is developing a life and personality of her own."

"Probably a very good thing. Allows you to be more creative."

"I agree. She needs a much stronger personality than mine."

He almost fell off the chair. "Right," he said, keeping a straight face. "A stronger personality than a Super-Avenger girl."

Now, it was her turn to laugh. "Oh, Brandon. This really is fun. When bad stuff happens later on, and it will, I hope we can remember some silly moments like this."

He stood and took her in his arms. "I hope we'll have lots of silly moments to choose from by then, hopefully a long time from now." She rose on tiptoe and he leaned down. Kissing her was such pleasure. He felt her love swim right through his being, but he caught himself before they went too far. He had paying clients to attend to in the morning.

"C'mon, sweetheart. We've got more work to do." He led her back to the table. "Since we're creating your brand, Kat, you need to be happy with what we do now. So let's look at a possible cover for the second book." He'd already designed a mock-up with the logo and series name and showed it to her alongside the first book. They looked darn good, and he visualized more to come. "What do you think?"

He didn't expect tears. Lots of them. How did this happen? One moment laughing, and the next...? Pushing the computer away, he took her hand. "What's wrong, Kat? None of my clients ever cried."

She just shook her head. "Nothing," she whispered. "It-it's perfect. Just perfect. But so real."

He kept listening, kicking himself. Totally in over his head. What did he miss along the way? Talk about clueless! If the design was that good, she should have been at least a little bit happy. "Maybe working together this way wasn't such a great idea," he finally said. "I can call one of my artist friends for you to work with instead."

"No!" She grasped his hands. "Brandon...it's scary. All of it. I've wanted this, and pictured this for so long, and now...I'm totally anxious, thrilled, amazed, frightened. I could go on."

Now he got it. "Afraid of success? Or afraid of failure?"

"Tissues. I need a tissue," she said, going to the counter to get some.

He waited, his heart sinking when she took the entire box back to the table.

She stayed standing, pacing a bit, as though she had too much energy to calm down. "I'm afraid of both, Bran. Success and failure." She flipped her hand in a motion of disgust. "So much for my rational mind that can solve quadradic equations. No help there."

When she got into range, he gently pulled her onto his lap. "Just talk to me."

She raised her head, wrapped her arms around his neck, and kissed him. "Thank you," she said. "For everything. All this work…the effort… No one else, not even Nonna, believes in me the way you do. You've actually brought to life—you've validated—this lonely road I've been on. You can't know how much that means to me. I love you for it."

A lot of responsibility seemed to rest on his shoulders. This was a side of Kathy he didn't know. So insecure. But he had to be honest. Her investment in time, energy, and emotion was too big to lead her down the wrong path.

"I enjoy designing for you, Kat, not because I want you to be happy, which of course I do, but because I liked your book. I've been around the publishing business, but from a design angle only. I'm not an editor or reviewer, so I'm no expert. I have a feeling, however, that if you continue writing, you'll find readers for your stories.

"If I had thought the book was terrible"—he shook his head—"I don't know exactly how I'd tell you, but I would not have done all this." He tapped the computer screen. "In all honesty, my love, I wouldn't have encouraged you."

He watched her absorb his words, her fingers steepled as she left his lap and stood.

"What would you have done instead?" she asked.

His mind raced. She'd gone to school for math, not writing. He'd spent years training in his field. Dozens of art and computer design courses. Degrees and certificates. "I would have told you to take writing classes," he finally said as he held his breath.

That sunshine smile appeared again, and he sighed in relief. "I'm a step ahead of you, Bran," she said. "How do you think I've gotten this far? I've been taking courses and workshops for the last four years, and I used to be in a critique group. Dana Moretti Mysteries have been the result."

He rose and twirled her around the kitchen, the dogs yapping at their feet. "I'm happy for you, Kat. I'm happy for us both. And I'm really happy you liked my ideas."

"Oh, I've gotten to like a lot of your ideas lately."

Hugging her close, he said, "How about we run with the dogs and try out a couple of those ideas afterwards?"

She nodded, blushed. "Another good time to savor."

"We're just starting out, sweetheart. We've got a lot of good times ahead."

##

On a late Sunday in January, Kathy sat at her kitchen table with Brandon and her parents, glad to finally have them meet.

"That was a good meal, Kathy. I'm happy the recipes came in handy, and I'm even happier that Dad and I are finally here."

Maybe that was true for her mom, but between the first handshake and sitting down to dinner, her dad and Brandon had been tiptoeing around each other like two boxers dancing in their respective corners. Now her dad sat opposite her, seemingly relaxed, as he leaned back in his chair. Maybe the hearty meal had mellowed him.

"Thanks, Mom. We're happy you came here, too. And as for your recipes...well, I think I finally figured out how to do pasta right."

She glanced quickly at Brandon, who tried to bury a chuckle. "Oh, she has her methods," he said.

Phone calls hadn't been enough for her folks. And her Christmas visit seemed like years ago to them. They were used to seeing her at least every weekend. With only one more chapter left to write in her current story, she'd invited them down, actually shocked they hadn't simply shown up before now on their own.

"So how about you come home next week," said Joe Russo, "and let Brandon meet your brothers. You're lucky they didn't come with us today. Your mother talked them out of it."

"I can just imagine, but they'll have to wait—"

"She hasn't finished that book yet," interrupted Marie. "That was the point of-of getting away. So don't nag at her, Joe."

Her folks had definitely been shaken up, maybe trying to understand. Maybe. "My writing schedule hasn't changed. I've got at least another month here, if not more." In fact, this might be a good time... She glanced at Brandon. He caught her eye and shrugged in a way that put the ball in her court.

"More?" echoed her mom. "What do you mean?"

"This is a nice town," Kathy replied. "We both like it here."

"What are you talking about, Kathy?" Her dad's voice was rising. "Where's here? This is a summer place. Good for vacations. Not a real place like Boston."

Laughing was not an option. "When I first got here, Dad, I thought exactly the same way. Living right on the beach is fantastic, even in winter. Getting to know a group of ROMEOs, adopting a couple of the cutest doggies, and meeting such wonderful people... I thought we were living in a magical place. Like in the *Wizard of Oz.* That it wasn't real."

"That's exactly what I'm saying. This is just a temporary place so you can get the writing out of your system."

She choked back a scream. *Come on, Brandon. Help me out.*

As though he read her mind, she heard, "But we learned, Mr. Russo, that Pilgrim Cove is as real as anyplace in the world. The vet's wife went into labor and we had to look after the dogs in his kennel, their preteen daughter needed our support. Then the storm came on New Year's, and we lost electricity for twenty-four hours. Despite all the adventures—and don't forget the original accident—we kept working our jobs full-time all the way through. If that's not real life, then what is?"

Her dad's eyes narrowed, and he looked at Marie. "Nonna did not do us any favors with this big idea. I don't like it. She's our only daughter, and I want her back in Boston."

"And I want her to be happy."

Like a deflated balloon, her dad slumped back. Kathy rushed to his side and took his hands. "I love you, Daddy. You're not going to lose me."

A gentle hand stroked her cheek, and she asked, "So how long did it actually take you to drive here?"

He shrugged. "An hour, maybe?"

"Is that really so bad? If I wound up in any of the Boston suburbs, it would take that long to get to your house. Traffic rules in Beantown, Dad. You know that."

Her mom started to clear the table. "I'll do it," said Brandon. He nodded at the door. "Why don't you take your folks for a walk on the beach? There's no wind today, and the hounds will appreciate it."

And give us some time alone. She glanced at her parents. "You guys up to it?"

They reached for their jackets. "Might as well get the lay of the land," grumbled Joe. "I'll take Sheba. She doesn't cause trouble!"

#

Surprisingly, her folks were quiet when they started walking on the hard sand. The dogs behaved, although her mom took the familiar Sheba while her dad handled Rocky and she kept Cleo with her. "Amazing how they get along."

"Rocky gets all the credit for introducing Bran and me." She'd mentioned the roadside rescue in passing, but now regaled them with the full account.

"Look at our daughter, Joe. Look how pretty, how animated." Her mom looped her arm with Kathy's. "Is he the one, sweetheart?"

Kathy halted, and suddenly tears threatened as she looked from her mom to her dad and back again. "Oh, yes. He is very much the one." She took a deep breath. "I'm thirty years old, not a child. But these feelings are new to me. I know how important family is to us, and I want so much for you to at least like him." She paused and added, "Affection and even love can come later."

Her mom kissed her, and Kathy looked at her father. "Dad, you won't succeed in scaring him off, so I hope…"

"If I scare him off, my Katarina, then he's not the one for you."

She guessed this was not the time to mention that Bran used the same words of affection. *My Katarina.*

"Ready to go back? I invited Bran's aunt and uncle for dessert. He has family, too."

"Then let's meet 'em."

She distributed plastic bags. "Not before this!"

##

"Showing them my new book designs was a genius move," said Kathy that night as they lay in bed.

"Genius? Hardly. It was a no-brainer. I had to get him on my side. What better way than to show him I'm on your side?"

She rolled over to see him better. "It was more than that," she said. "I didn't hear another word about getting the writing 'out of my system.' Maybe they finally understand that it's part of me." She sighed. "A part that doesn't pay well."

"Not yet, but later on…who knows?

"Hmm…" he said, clearing his throat. "How do you feel about getting in touch with Quinn's granddaughter, Lila, and asking about rentals here? All-year-round rentals?"

Her breath caught. "Just a sec. Reality check coming." She plumped her pillows, sat up, and stretched her fingers out, ready to count off. Then plopped her arm down. "You know, I can't think of anything other than we're a bit farther away from my folks and yours. I usually go into Mass Life once or twice a month, but no big deal."

"I visit new clients at their convenience—any time, weekdays or weekends. Being self-employed requires that flexibility. But even so, I don't see any issues. Especially with the ferry service as another option."

"Right! I forgot all about that."

"It takes you into Rowes Wharf at Harborside. We could catch the T from there to go anywhere in town."

She remained quiet for a moment. "This is a big step, Bran. Really taking it to the next level."

He put out his hand. "I'm already there."

She twined her fingers through his. "Yes. Call her."

LINDA BARRETT

CHAPTER THIRTEEN

Kathy stared at the words on her computer screen, where Dana Moretti had successfully solved another case by coupling opportunity and motive with a little geometry, trigonometry, and common sense. *A Calculated Incident?* Absolutely. Her character's favorite kind. A delicious combination of math and mystery. Kathy loved putting it together.

She placed her hands back on the keyboard, centered her cursor, and typed *The End* after the last line of text. She'd finished with a week to spare for revision. Deadline met. Perfect.

She couldn't sit still and waltzed around the room, simply celebrating a bit. She glanced at the clock, itching to tell Brandon. "I'll be right back," she said to her four-legged companions, and grabbing a sweater, she ran downstairs.

His kitchen door was always left open, and she walked in to see Bran standing in the room. Of course, he'd heard her footsteps as she ran and expected her to appear. But now he held up his hand to wait, and she saw the phone against his ear, his eyes alert as he nodded every so often. He walked back into the dining room, checking his calendar—a large paper calendar.

"Tuesday, the eleventh, one o'clock in your office. I'll be there… Absolutely, I'll bring some general ideas, and show you what I've already done for others." He disconnected, and Kathy saw a big smile cross his face.

"New client?" she asked.

"Hopefully. A commercial account, just what I need to grow my own portfolio." He winked. "I'll be taking that ferry into Rowes Wharf."

She opened her arms, and he walked into them, hugging her back.

"We can both celebrate," she said, twirling away from him. "I finished the book! Dana Moretti is on her way to a third adventure!"

"Congratulations! We'll have to put finishing touches on your website."

She squeezed his hand, so grateful he remembered without her having to ask, but not wanting to distract him from his paid work. "I can wait. I still have to revise and send it to the copyeditor to ferret out typos and other mistakes. But I am so psyched for us. Let's go out to dinner."

A smile lurked; his eyes twinkled. "No more lobster! I don't have the time."

"Then we'll celebrate next week, after your visit to the new client."

"Potential client," he corrected. "Let's hope it works out, so we can afford that lobster as well as a place to live here. Did I mention Lila's call this morning?"

"No-o-o." Her heart raced. "Tell me, tell me! I love the idea."

"Me, too. She wants to talk with us, find out about our budget, where we'd like to live, and all those details. She knows her stuff and didn't make any promises."

"That's because there's probably very little available." She walked closer and took his hand. "Living on the beach is rare, even in this town. Some people live on the bay, some live away from all water. That's why Sea View House is special."

She looked over where Rocky lay. "I don't think we'll get this lucky again."

"We're already lucky, Kat. No matter what."

She snuggled against his chest and felt his arms go around her. "You're right, of course. I love a man whose glass is half-full." She kissed him quickly and walked toward the door. "Finish up your business day while I go browse the internet for real estate in Pilgrim Cove. Just to get a feel."

"Great idea. Then we can get some burgers at the diner."

She gave him a thumbs-up and disappeared.

When he knocked on her door an hour later, she greeted him with a heavier heart. "We'd better enjoy Sea View House every minute we're here. That foundation made our rent very reasonable. We can't afford anything I saw online."

"Really? We both earn a decent living."

True enough, but… "Let's put it another way," she said. "I don't want to pay out that much money in rent with no investment behind it. It's like throwing money into the wind."

"Maybe we can figure something out with Lila. Don't worry about it. C'mon, I'm hungry."

"Fill his stomach and he's good to go," she teased. "If only every problem was so easily solved."

##

"A final word to the wise, Kathy. The company wants everyone full-time in the very near future. No one will be thirty hours anymore. I advise you to consider that while you think about what I asked you. It's a great opportunity. Let me know by tomorrow."

"I will, Elizabeth. Thank you."

What else could she say? Kathy looked at the phone, placed it on the table, and just sat still, reeling from her conversation with her boss. She was flattered, of course. Elizabeth had just offered Kathy not only a promotion to supervising the projects of newer employees, but a raise in salary, which was not insignificant.

Jumping from her chair, she started her usual pacing and calculating the plusses and minuses. A load of plusses. Challenging work, more money, nice people who spoke the same language as she. Accepting it should have been a no-brainer. It would have been under normal circumstances.

But when would she have time to write? She'd worked so hard on this second career. Even defied her family by moving away to make this dream of hers come true. She'd been on her own since college, making her way, paying her bills. *Where there's a will, there's a way.* She believed that mantra—right until now. Now she wasn't sure about anything except that it was her decision, not Brandon's. She had to be rational. After investing time and energy to establish an independent life, how could she choose writing and allow herself to be dependent on Bran? Not fair to him. She wanted a loving relationship of equals.

She walked to the kitchen window and stared at the ocean next door. On this sunny day, the waves sparkled with diamond peaks. Over and over, they rose on the horizon and finally crashed to the shore. The longer she continued watching, the calmer she felt. Finally, she nodded. "Nothing stays the same," she voiced out loud, "except you."

Too bad they'd wasted Lila's time on Saturday. Pilgrim Cove was out of the picture. Worse, so was Dana Moretti in her bright red sweater. Kathy squeezed her eyes closed as a corner of her heart ripped with pain. Bran would be so disappointed. She wrapped her arms around her stomach and allowed herself to grieve.

##

When he returned home from Boston on Tuesday afternoon, Brandon glanced at his calendar, picked up the phone, and made a reservation at the Wayside Inn for Friday night. Valentine's Day. He wasn't going to make the same mistake twice. Looking back, of course, New Year's Eve had turned out just fine, but this time they'd be celebrating in style. Flowers, dinner, dancing…a great time with the one he loved. And perhaps some friends.

Whistling for Rocky, he texted Kat to walk the dogs. He had good news, which he hoped would cheer her up. She hadn't seemed herself yesterday but wouldn't say why. Maybe just an off day. He was definitely not an expert on women.

Her smile was back. Lipstick, too.

He sighed with relief and greeted her with wave and a smile of his own. "Are you up to a jog? These pups look ready to run."

"Are you kidding? Let's go."

The beach was barren at that time of day, in that season. Not as appealing to most people, but with a beauty of its own. One day, he'd scratch his itch to capture it on paper or use a camera. He'd never get tired of the seashore. When they eventually slowed down to a walk, he asked, "Aren't you curious?"

"Of course I am, but I figured you'd tell me when you were ready." She glanced at her watch. "As long as it didn't take more than another ten minutes!"

There was no one like her. Supergirl. Avenger girl. "Kathy, my love…you are one in a million. Yes, we can celebrate. I now have a new client who wants me to work on several projects that will—and I quote—captivate consumers. Computer and print. Advertisements, brochures, logos. A retail operation. Good for our bottom line."

"Wonderful, Bran. You must have wowed them. I'm happy for you."

"And by the way, taking the ferry was a hoot."

"I can just imagine. No traffic all the way to Boston." A quick smile that faded just as quickly.

His instincts kicked in again. Something was off. And not just a bad day.

"Okay, Katarina. Are you going to tell me what's going on? You're not yourself."

He watched as she stopped walking and stared at the Atlantic before reaching for his hand.

"I've got some news, too."

Her sadness, her voice. "Oh, God, Kat. Are you sick? Is someone ill? Your mom? Nonna?"

She jumped as though pulled by marionette strings. "No, no. Nothing like that. I'm sorry. Boy, I really must sound awful to scare you that way."

"Now that I can breathe again, talk to me."

"Well, things are changing at Mass Life. I accepted a promotion today—full-time, part of management." She pivoted to face him. "I'm so sorry, Bran. This…this Pilgrim Cove thing isn't going to work out. I have to be in Boston every day."

"So?"

"So?" she repeated and couldn't have looked more astonished.

He touched his forehead to hers. "We're a team, Katarina. Did you think I'd choose the beach over you?"

"I-I didn't think of that, only of how disappointed you'd be. I was surprised that Lila was somewhat encouraging on Saturday and…you looked so happy." She stepped back. "I just can't figure out how to fix this! How to fix anything this time." She inhaled so deeply he heard her. "Especially the Dana stories."

Dana. The books she loved writing. There lay the crux of all this. "Tell me more." Which was exactly a prompt he used with clients in order to understand them better.

She didn't answer right away, just kept looking at the water, the sky with the incoming clouds, the stretch of beach. "There's only twenty-four hours in a day," she said quietly. "How can I do everything? I had it all going so well."

"But you can't control the world, my love. Listen up. We can fix Dana. I've got ideas about the timeline, and you're not killing her off. Aside from that, and more important—" He took a breath, gazed at the sky, then back at Kathy.

"You know what I think?" he asked, gesturing toward the house, the sand, the ocean, and its distant horizon. "I think we both fell for it. Despite being so smart and savvy."

They'd reached the big house and let themselves and the dogs in. She hadn't said a word since he'd spoken. Until finally, she raised her head. In her eyes, he saw curiosity.

"You mean, we both fell for all the Bart Quinn magical stuff?"

"Exactly," he said with a curt nod. "Oh, we worked hard to convince your folks otherwise. We worked hard to convince ourselves, too. But…I sure wasn't looking for a relationship when I moved here."

"And I just wanted a quiet place to write and work." She slowly removed her jacket but kept her eyes on him. "Maybe, just maybe, deep inside both of us," she whispered, "we wanted to believe him. Our very sophisticated selves still wanted the magic, needed a little magic, so we lived in this fantasy."

"Yeah…"

"Until now, when we got shot down."

His heart almost stopped. Did she mean they were broken, too? He couldn't let that happen. "It depends on the real dream, Katarina. Not the fantasy."

Her eyes met his immediately. "When you say my true name…it always sounds special."

"I love your name in all its guises. I love holding you in my arms, and I love kissing your beautiful mouth. I just love you, period!" His pulse raced; his breath was shallow. He felt as though he'd just run a mile up the beach and back again. "Is that enough basis for a dream come true, Katarina? A forever dream of the heart?"

Her mouth opened and closed. A quizzical but hopeful expression. She coughed. "Are you…"

He hadn't planned it. He hadn't bought a ring. He hadn't introduced her to his folks. He didn't care about any of it.

"I am. I certainly am."

She few into his arms. "The answer is yes."

"You're my dream, sweetheart. We'll just take the magic with us wherever we go and build our lives with it."

"Maybe that's what the old leprechaun with his gift of gab was trying to tell us," Kathy added. "The magic only begins here, and then…whoosh, we're on our own."

Brandon let his gaze drift around the room until it rested on Rocky. He motioned him over and bent down to rub behind his ears. The dog crooned.

"Here's where our magic began," Brandon said. "A little roadside rescue, which turned into a little family. Can't ask for more than that."

"Amen," added the woman with the killer smile.

He rose and took her in his arms, exactly where she belonged.

##

They might not have had time to buy the ring yet, but Brandon wasn't letting Valentine's Day go to waste. Flowers at home, dinner and dancing at the Wayside Inn. He'd put a call out to the new friends they'd made in town to join them if possible. He'd called a few other folks as well.

And it seemed the locals all wanted a night out.

He and Kathy stood in the bar area with Adam and Becca, their first outing in two months.

"We have a babysitter," said the new mom. "Sara is insulted, actually. But I couldn't possibly make her totally responsible."

Lila and Jason Parker approached. "We're getting demerits for deserting the good ship Lobster Pot," Lila said, "but this was special. We wanted to be here."

Brandon shook hands with the man. "Glad to finally meet you. Katie is quite the firecracker."

Jason rolled his eyes. "Don't I know it. But there's hope yet for the younger one!"

Another couple approached, waving to Lila. "Thanks for including us," said the slender brunette. "We needed a break, and couldn't wait to meet the current tenants."

Brandon laughed and introduced himself and Kathy.

"I'm Rachel Levine." She extended her hand to each of them. "My husband, Jack, and I started out in Sea View House, too. Bart doesn't miss an opportunity to…let's see how to say this…to arrange things to his liking." She nodded. "Yes, indeed, Quinn does meddle. You can read about us in that journal he insisted we write in."

"The entries are short, sweet, and…a little sappy," Jack whispered. "But it makes Bart happy."

"Ah, Bart Quinn. He's here even when in Florida," said Brandon.

"He certainly is," said Lila, turning toward Brandon. "In fact, he reminded me about a possible property for you both. A small bungalow at the end of the bay."

Instantly, Kathy's smile quivered, and Brandon hugged her close. However, his Supergirl forged on. "I'm so sorry, Lila, and very disappointed, but our plans have changed. I'll be working in Boston full-time starting next month, so…"

"So, what's that got to do with the price of bread?" asked the Realtor before turning to the others. "Hey, Jack, Jason," she called, "tell these people how most of the Cove commutes to Beantown every single day and are never late for work."

"She's right." A manly chorus.

"The ferry has an over ninety-nine percent on-time rate. Go compare that to sitting behind the wheel in traffic!" Lila's blue eyes sparkled like champagne bubbles. A real estate maven who knew her town.

"I told Kat that the ferry was a fun ride," said Brandon, "but I never inquired about the year-round service."

"Thirty minutes each way," said Jack. "Every hour and half hour. And you can catch the T a couple of blocks from the wharf if you need it."

"Right. I've done that already," said Brandon, as Kathy turned in his arms. With her eyes opened wide, she said, "What do you think?"

"You tell me," he said. "You're the one commuting, so you…"

"Then I say, let's look at the house. Let's try."

As he leaned down to kiss her, two more familiar couples caught his eye. "Brace yourself, Kat. My folks just showed up, with my aunt and uncle."

"Why didn't you tell me they were coming?"

"You had enough on your mind, and I wasn't sure they'd get here in time tonight anyway."

"I heard that," said the tall man who had to be Brandon's dad. So similar, it was like seeing a future version of Bran. "Nothing would keep us away from meeting Kathy." He clapped Brandon on the shoulder, then opened his arms to greet her. "Ralph and Linda have kept us posted, and we've been jealous!"

"Hello, Kathy," said Brandon's mom, reaching for a hug. "You've made my son a very happy man. So welcome to the family."

"That was so easy," whispered Kathy as she turned to Brandon.

Ralph laughed a hearty deep sound. "We ROMEOs know how to do it right."

Brandon checked the entranceway again. He'd hoped one other couple would show up on this significant evening. And, ah-h…just coming in the door…two familiar faces and…more?

"Another surprise, Kat," he whispered. "Take a look who's walking over."

"Oh, my God," she breathed before running to greet her parents. "What a surprise." She turned toward her brothers and sister-in-law. "You're all here."

"Of course we're all here," said Joey. "We've got to check the dude out."

Her two other brothers stood on either side of Joe. Jennifer shrugged in a *what can I do?* sort of way.

"Did you think you could just decide to marry someone without us knowing him?" added Nicky.

Kathy seemed overwhelmed. Brandon gently urged her toward him and turned to her brothers. "You will have a lifetime to check me out, bros. Our door will always be open to you and the entire family. I'm not going anywhere without her."

"This is all too funny," said Kathy. "I came to Pilgrim Cove to get away from family for a while. And now the family's doubled in size! And I'm happy about it." She searched each one. "If Nonna were here, this party would be perfect."

Marie handed her a cell phone. "FaceTime, sweetheart. Say hello."

Kathy grabbed the phone from her mom. "Nonna! It's good to see you, even on a small screen. You're going to love Brandon. I fell head over heels in no time."

"When it's the right person, my Katarina, that's what happens. Like your grandfather and me. Now let me see this man of yours."

Brandon took the phone and looked into the face of a grandmother every child should know. A face of love.

"Hi, Nonna. I'm so happy to finally meet you. Katarina talks about you all the time, and I want you to know how blessed I feel to have found her."

"Now that makes me feel better. My granddaughter lives in my heart, Brandon. Her happiness is everything to me. So love each other. Be kind to each other. Support each other. Make sure she's picked the right man."

The woman packed a verbal punch, but she got to the heart of the matter.

"You won't be disappointed, Nonna. I promise you that." He looked at the crowd and spoke into the phone. "Can you stay on the line another minute. We're going to make a toast."

"I have my wine right here, young man. And so do Bart and Honey."

Brandon chuckled as he lifted his arm. "Attention everyone, please. Glasses up as I propose a toast to my most loving, beautiful, intelligent, brave, dog-loving bride-to-be, and to all of you, the friends we made here and to our families, who appreciated a night out with the ones they love.

"Happy Valentine's Day, everyone!"

SEA VIEW HOUSE JOURNAL

(Pilgrim Cove Series)

From Laura McCloud Parker – I arrived at Sea View House in March, looking for a place to catch my breath and get on with life. I'd just lost my mom and completed my own breast cancer treatment, one event right after the other. The first person I met in Pilgrim Cove, besides Bart Quinn, was Matt Parker. And the first part of him I saw was his jeans and work boots, sticking out from beneath my kitchen sink. "Hand me the wrench," he said, thinking I was his son. How could I have known then that living in this ***House on the Beach*** would forever change my life? Bart says it's a magical place. I'm not arguing.....

From Shelley Anderson Stone– The children and I arrived at Sea View House on Memorial Day weekend. Divorce hurts everybody, and we all needed time to recover. Bart Quinn had given us the large apartment downstairs called The Captain's Quarters. I had no idea that Daniel Stone would be living upstairs in the Crow's Nest, dealing with his own grief. I also had no idea he would rock my world—in the very best of ways—and that we'd provide each other with a second chance at love. Looking back, I can say that season was *No Ordinary Summer* for any of us....

From Daniel Stone – Read Shelley's account. Here's my P.S. – if there's any magic at all, it was provided by Jessie, my golden retriever. Two little kids and a golden? Pure magic.

From Rachel Goodman Levine – Like a prodigal daughter, I returned to my home town of Pilgrim Cove in the fall, trying to prove myself as an assistant principal of the high school. Instead of living with my folks, I landed at Sea View House. I wasn't alone there. Thank you, Bart Quinn! Marine biologist Jack Levine had settled into the Crow's Nest. My initial delight turned to dismay when Jack joined my teaching staff, breaking all the rules with his unorthodox methods. And getting me into trouble. It was then the magic happened. The discovery. The love. Somehow, we *Reluctant Housemates* are now housemates forever right here in Pilgrim Cove....

From Jack Levine – Read Rachel's story. All I'll say is: magic my eye! Sure, I'll admit that sailors are a superstitious bunch. But here's what really happened: my boat went missing and shook her up. It wasn't magic. It was a miracle! All of it. So believe what you want.

From Jason Parker – I came back after nine years because I couldn't outrun the pain. Prom night. A car wreck. My twin brother gone. Our music gone with him. Except not. I've got platinum behind me, and what does it mean? Nothing without the folks I love. Less than nothing without Lila Sullivan. She's always been the one, the only one for me. Bless Bart Quinn for lending me Sea View House. My daughter was conceived there a long time ago. But I didn't know anything about her during all those years. Folks might call Katie *The Daughter He Never Knew,* and they'd be right. But I know her now. As for her mom and me…? Sea View House came through for us again. Our wedding took place right there. I believe in the magic. I believe in happily ever after. If that's not love, what is?

From Lila Sullivan – Read Jason's account. All I'll add is that the right girl for lovely Adam Fielding is still out there. Jason's return saved Adam and me from a tepid marriage of convenience. We both deserved more. My money's on Adam and Sea View House.

(Sea View House Series)

From Rebecca Hart Fielding – It's summer again, a year since the last entry in this journal. The magic is still here. In this place, in this town, in its people. After the Boston Marathon, I arrived at Sea View House with no expectations except to focus on rehab. I wanted to hide, but that's impossible in Pilgrim Cove. In a nutshell, I met Adam in a bar. A nice bar at the Wayside Inn. It was definitely NOT love at first sight. But something changed along the way.

From Adam Fielding – We fell in love. That's what happened. That's the magic everyone talks about. No woo-woo. No smoke and mirrors. Scientists don't believe in that stuff. When Becca came to Sea View House, all she wanted to do was walk again. She was stubborn. She was proud. And she was determined to remain the athlete she'd always been. I'm happy to say that ***Her Long Walk Home*** brought her straight into my arms.

From Joy MacKenzie Nash – If anyone needed the magic of Sea View House, it was Logan and me. He didn't believe in it, of course. But grief lived in my heart, and I was open to anything. How ironic that this kindergarten teacher couldn't have her own children. I pretended to be happy. Maybe I overdid the act. When Logan met me, he thought I was a ditz, and I thought he was the loneliest person I'd ever met, always hiding behind his camera.

From Logan Nash – Love stared at me through the lens of my Nikon. Joy, Joy, Joy. She was everywhere. But what I did I know about love? Nothing. I was a foster care kid, never dreaming of a family of my own, not even knowing how an ordinary family worked. And the magic? When Joy said yes, her eyes shining with love, I knew that between us, she'd get ***Her Picture-Perfect Family.*** And so would I. That's magic enough for me.

From Alison Berg-Romano – After my husband died, I wasn't looking for another love or another hero. The grief and guilt following his death haunted me. All I wanted was a safe, quiet life, a private life away from the city. I took my infant son and rented a house in cozy Pilgrim Cove. Little did I know Mike Romano lived across the street. Mike didn't believe in quiet. Or solitude. Or privacy. He drove me crazy until I saw the truth. He was my cheering section. My go-to guy. He had my back. And his eyes shone with love when he looked my way. But not even for me would he stop fighting fires in Pilgrim Cove.

From Mike Romano – Starting over is not easy, but Ali is much stronger than she thinks. All I did was nag and tease and challenge her—and play with baby Joey—until she finally agreed to a dinner date. I'm sure she just wanted to shut me up and live her quiet life again. But I couldn't let that happen. She's too brave, beautiful, and talented to give up on life. In her, I saw myself, no stranger to second chances. Her husband was a hero, and I'm certainly not qualified as ***Her Second-Chance Hero.*** I'm just a guy giving back to the town I love. And to the woman who stole my heart.

From Kathy Russo – All I wanted was a quiet place to write. No family. No neighbors. No interruptions. Peace and quiet would be magic enough for me! With my grandmother's rescue dog, Sheba, for company, the upstairs unit at Sea View House was perfect. Even in winter, with the mighty Atlantic next door, a house on the beach is a treat. I had no idea I'd run into trouble before I'd even arrived.

From Brandon Bigelow – It should have been easy. An off-season rental on the beach should have been a perfect place to rebuild my business and figure out where to live next. I hadn't counted on meeting Kathy Russo on my way into town and becoming one of ***Her Roadside Rescues*** along with my new dog, Rocky. Somehow peace and quiet doesn't have a chance when a couple of rescues are involved. And a man doesn't have a chance when looking into the sparking eyes of a petite woman who thinks she's a superhero. Neither of us believed in the tales of magic that went with the place. But we didn't have to. Finding each other was magic enough.

From Bartholomew Quinn – *It's all about the magic.* That's the truth, but these young people refuse to admit it. So let's be scientific. What do these loving couples have in common? **Sea View House!** Is it mere coincidence that, in recent times, eight couples met there, fell in love, and got married afterwards? No! It's *not* a coincidence. The sun, sand, and ocean might provide the perfect atmosphere, but in the end, it's the magic.

Sea View House has been an enchanted hideaway from the beginning. A special place to heal. Or a place to solve life's problems. I expect the powers of Sea View House will continue long after I'm gone. But to tell the truth, I've got no plans to go anywhere yet…except to Florida for a winter break. I'm going with a gal who likes my company. A gal who made this old heart race like a young stallion's. But I can also see that Honeybelle's eyes gleam when I look her way. It seems the Sea View House charm is not only for the young but for the young at heart. Did I mention that Honeybelle MacKenzie happened to live there for a while?

Imagine! After all this time, the magic's come around to touch me! And it's still there.

HELLO FROM LINDA

Dear Reader—

Thank you so much for choosing to read *Her Roadside Rescues,* the fourth book of my Sea View House series. I hope you enjoyed your visit to Pilgrim Cove where a love story always unfolds for the tenants of Sea View House. If this was your first visit to Pilgrim Cove and you'd like to read more stories, you can find them all at your favorite bookseller. An excerpt from Book 1, *Her Long Walk Home* follows this letter. This book is free! I hope those of you who've read the prior books in the series enjoyed a visit with old friends.

I've also provided an excerpt from the first book in the related *Pilgrim Cove* series. *The House on the Beach* is an award-winning story that readers have fervently praised. That book is also free!

If you enjoyed *Her Roadside Rescues,* I'd truly appreciate you helping others find it so they can discover Linda Barrett books, too. Here's what you can do:

*Write an honest review and post it on the site where you purchased it.
*Sign up for my newsletter on my website.
*Visit my website at: www.linda-barrett.com. See what's new!
*Tell your friends! The best book recommendations come from friends because we trust them!

Thanks again for reading and for helping to get the word out. I truly appreciate you.

Best always,
Linda

EXCERPT FROM
HER LONG WALK HOME
(SEA VIEW HOUSE SERIES BOOK ONE)

"Will she use the ramp or try the stairs?"

Bartholomew Quinn, proud founder and co-president of Quinn Real Estate and Property Management, leaned forward in his oversized leather chair and peered through the large front window of his Main Street office. A young woman faced the building, her dark hair neatly gathered behind her neck. She wore a long dark skirt and a red sweater. In her right hand, she held a cane. Bart watched her glance flicker between the two paths. Ramp or stairs? Either might be considered a challenge for her, but... He caught her determined expression as she made her choice.

Quickly transferring the cane, the woman placed her right hand on the railing. Her chin jutted forward as she raised her right foot to the first step, her left following only a tad more slowly.

"Atta girl," he cheered.

Quinn had become familiar with this girl's background through a trustworthy friend. Now he'd seen her in action for himself. In a moment, he'd depend on his gut instinct to fill in the blanks. He'd been blessed with the knack, those "people skills" folks talked about, and those instincts had never let him down. He'd know Rebecca Hart well by the time their conversation was over.

A sea breeze brought the flavor of the ocean to Bart's nose, and he inhaled with joy. Another summer season was poised to begin in Pilgrim Cove, his favorite place on earth. He'd spent his entire adult life here, and he'd be buried here—God willing—many years from now. He was young! Seventy-six years young, and people in this town depended on him.

He and his buddies had come through every time. They made themselves available to meet, greet, and befriend newcomers as well as summer folk. Or, as his granddaughter Lila would say, they were always ready to meddle—especially him. Well, his lassie might have a point. But he wasn't so sure. So far, all his "meddling" had turned out well.

And now, Rebecca Hart had come to see him. His anticipation sizzled as he walked down the hallway to greet her. Hopefully, Sea View House would be sheltering a new resident.

#

Becca hid her smile as she evaluated Bart Quinn. The old guy had definitely kissed the Blarney Stone more than a few times, but he still had it—that courtesy of his generation. A true gentleman. He'd put her at ease immediately and treated her as though she were like anyone else. As though she hadn't been watching the runners at the finish line in Boston instead of running herself. As though the marathon had never happened. Except, of course, it had, and she wasn't one to wear rose-colored glasses. Leaning across Quinn's desk, Becca stared directly at him, commanding his full attention.

"My cousin, Josie, and I checked into the Wayside Inn last night, but I can't afford to stay there much longer. So I'd like to see this house you have where the rent is so reasonable it has to be a mistake." If there was a mix-up, she'd need to find another place right away. "My graduate professor at BU insisted I contact you. He said his colleague at Harvard had some clout with this office. Is that true?"

The light in Quinn's blue eyes rivaled the light of the sun. It sparkled and blazed as he rubbed his hands together. Becca sat hypnotized. Was Quinn a man or an oversized leprechaun? His fist banged the arm of his chair.

"You're talking about Daniel Stone! We call him the Professor. Comes back every year since his first summer in Pilgrim Cove. Now that was a story… Was it last year or the one before that, when he stayed at Sea View House? He'd lost his wife, ya see, and was in a grievous state." Quinn's head moved from side to side as he made sorrowful sounds. "I gave him the upstairs apartment, the Crow's Nest. But waiting for him downstairs was Shelley Anderson and her two little tykes. Ahh. That was no ordinary summer, no sirree. And now they're a family, everybody together."

His index finger pointed directly at her. "Sea View House holds the magic."

Magic? Baloney. She'd bet her last nickel the man could regale her with stories until the sun went down. She didn't have time for stories.

"Very nice, Mr. Quinn. But what I need to know is whether you've got a cottage for me to rent this summer. Easy access would be needed."

"True enough, lassie. But you did well coming up those steps. I watched from that window." He pointed behind him.

Her body stiffened. "You spied on me?" She adjusted her angle slightly to peer over his shoulder. Sure enough, she saw a swath of Main Street through the glass. She looked at Quinn again and sighed. "Why am I not surprised? I bet you don't miss much around here."

"You'd win that bet, my girl. This town is special to me. And will be to you, too."

"You mean you've got a place for rent? A house that will suit me?"

"Haven't you been listening, lass?"

He posed the question with such wide-eyed innocence that her lips twitched. Between the irascible Bart Quinn and her own one-track mind, she was in no better position than Alice was in Wonderland. The twitch became a smile, then a giggle, and she found herself laughing aloud, as though she'd finally gotten the joke.

And then the tears fell.

She reached for the tissue box Quinn slid toward her and dabbed her eyes. Strange that she wasn't embarrassed. "Well, that was a first."

"The laughing?"

"No. The crying."

The man seemed surprised.

"They have meds for the physical pain, Mr. Quinn. No tears there. As for the rest, well, as my mother taught me from the beginning: *Life hurts. Deal with it.*"

After studying her for a moment, Bart Quinn finally said, "Well, now, respecting all mothers, of course, I've got a different slant. I say, *Grab the brass ring and enjoy the ride."* He rose from his seat, rummaged through a drawer, and soon dangled a set of keys. "Let's go, my dear."

"Go where?"

"Where else would I bring a friend of a friend of Daniel Stone's than to Sea View House? Right beside the ocean, where you'll hear the sound of the surf, the call of the gulls, and where you'll find your own healing."

#

Becca was about to tell him that her healing came from physical therapy, not from ocean waves, when two small tornadoes blew into the room. The first was blonde, her long hair woven into a French braid that probably started the day neatly plaited. The other whirlwind sported dark waves framing a sweet face. Cinderella and Snow White. Totally adorable.

"Guess what, Papa Bart!" said Cinderella. "No school till Tuesday 'cause of the holiday, so Sara can sleep over." The child's infectious grin coupled with her attitude easily confirmed her as a twig on Bart Quinn's family tree.

Sara stepped forward. "If that's okay," she added quietly.

This girl's entrance had been embellished by her friend. Sara seemed more reserved and sensitive. A classic dark-eyed beauty who'd mature into a stunning woman one day.

"Sara, my girl," began Bart, "would you condemn me to a quiet house when we could be playing a hot game of...of"—Quinn glanced at Becca then back at the child—"Candy Land instead?"

A frown lined Sara's brow. "Candy Land?" she asked, her voice laced with incredulity. "That's for babies. Poker is more fun. Isn't your penny jar still full?"

Quinn looked at the ceiling, then at the girls. "Ach. What will Ms. Rebecca think of us now? You've gotten us in trouble, you have." He looked at Becca. Two other pairs of eyes followed suit. "Better a round of cards than leaving them to their little computer machines all night. Agree or not?"

Oh, she agreed. These children couldn't appreciate their good luck. A loving grandfather, probably good parents, too. Even the quieter one knew she was welcome here in the middle of a business day. Secure, confident children. They'd have no idea how other kids lived. Kids who hoarded a penny. Kids with no dads or granddads. Kids with a mom who worked all the time. Kids like Becca.

She couldn't have found better entertainment than Bart Quinn and the girls if she'd paid for a ticket of admission. But she hadn't come to be entertained. She tapped her watch. "Your granddaughters are delightful," she said. "But time is flying." Bracing her hands on the arms of the chair, she stood, took a moment to find her balance, and reached for her cane. "I'm ready when you are."

"I've been ready since the day I was born," said Quinn. Turning toward the little blonde, he said, "Katie, love, tell your mom I'm away to..."

A pretty blonde woman, definitely Katie's mom and definitely pregnant, walked into the room at a good clip, a leather tote bag on her arm.

"Wherever it is," she said, "you'll have to take the girls. I'm showing the Bascomb property on the bay, and then I've got a doctor's appointment, which I must keep or feel Jason's wrath."

"If you don't mind," said Becca, "I'll be waiting in my car—right out front." She'd have considered another Realtor at this point if her curiosity about Sea View House hadn't been piqued. Not to mention that low, low rent. And if she'd known another Realtor. The kids were cute, but really, was this any way to run a business?

As if she read her thoughts, the other woman smiled and extended her hand. "Hi there. I'm Lila Parker, Chief Cook and Bottle Washer around here. Where's my granddad taking you today?"

Becca shook her hand, glad to see no sign of pity or sympathy. "He calls it Sea View House."

Lila's brows hit her hairline, her eyes widened to saucer size, but a small grin started to emerge, too. "Perfect. It's a special place." She cocked her head toward Bart. "He's in charge of that property, never tells me about possible residents. It's all hush-hush until it's done."

Becca didn't care about mysteries, but walking was easier than standing, and she stepped toward the door. "I'll let you know how special it is…if I ever get there."

"I hear ya." Bart and the girls followed her. Once outside, the man installed the kids into the backseat of his decade-old Lincoln Town Car and opened the front passenger door for Becca.

"Honestly, Mr. Quinn, it's easier for me to drive. That is, to get into the car on the driver's side. My right leg's fine."

"Then I'll keep you in my mirror. We'll take it slow so you can look around as we travel."

Becca opened her door and threw her purse inside. She'd left the seat in the far back position she'd used to exit the car. Now she'd have enough room to manipulate her prosthetic left leg while getting in. She sat down facing the street, then turned and shifted her weight toward the front, her right leg going inside. She guided the left. The sequence made sense. Her physical therapy was paying off, and she'd be continuing it in Boston and at the medical clinic in Pilgrim Cove. If this house worked out. Or if Quinn had something else.

With a little luck, forethought, and care, she'd become the woman she once was. She'd become whole again. Or almost. Whole enough for a marathon? Whew. If only… She chased the thought away. More important on the survival scale was a job. As a respiratory therapist at Mass General, she'd needed strong legs to run around the halls, treating patients on every floor. She'd been building a career at the prestigious hospital, with two promotions behind her and supervisory responsibilities on her plate, too.

Now her small savings would trickle away in no time. There was a tiny chance, of course, that she'd receive some money from that charity fund set up after the marathon. But how much could that be? A few dollars? Even a few thousand wouldn't make a real difference in the long run. She'd have to rely only on herself. Her finances were tighter than a balloon's knot. A reality that tied her stomach into a dozen knots.

As promised, Quinn drove slowly, providing her with that opportunity to look around. From the man's office on Main Street, she passed a bank, a barber shop, and the nautically designed Diner on the Dunes. She spotted Parker Plumbing and Hardware. The name seemed familiar. That Lila woman? Then she saw the beautiful greyhound—on a leash. She glanced up. At the other end of the leash stood a tall, built, nice-looking guy. Behind the pair was a pet store with a big sign in the window. Adoption Day. Whew! A greyhound. Talk about running…

She followed Bart left onto Outlook Drive and made another left onto Beach Street. He tooted his horn, pointed out the window, and eased into a driveway. Becca slowed down, scanned the street, and took her time before pulling in behind him.

She hadn't known what to expect, but Sea View House was bigger than anything she'd imagined or could care for. Salt-box style. Weathered wood. A large sloping roof. Two stories with a third window above…maybe an attic. A white wooden fence surrounded the front yard on Beach Street.

Disappointment flooded her. What was the man thinking? She could never take care of a house like that. She hoped Quinn had another property to show her. Something small and easy. She rolled down her window and remained inside the car. With her first breath, she tasted the flavor of ocean and sea grass. She inhaled again, more deeply this time. No mistaking that definitive aroma existing only at the shore.

She looked again at the big house. A house right on the beach. Not that she'd swim… How could she? But she'd hear the waves. She'd see them, too. And that view…the pleasure of that view…that elusive horizon where ocean meets sky. Tempting. Oh, so tempting. So different from the confines of a hospital rehab wing, where she'd spent the last five weeks working to recover.

"Needing some assistance after all, lassie?" Quinn was at her car door.

"What else do you have to show me?"

And with that question, she'd reduced Bart Quinn to silence.

So what if she'd jumped to conclusions? The house was divided into two apartments, as Quinn had mentioned in his story of the professor. The Realtor had the first floor in mind for Becca. While Sara and Katie scurried ahead, Becca walked more slowly down the paved driveway to the back of the house. And came to an abrupt halt when she saw the ocean. The mighty Atlantic would be her closest neighbor. Not a rabbit hole, this time. Paradise.

She noted the spacious covered porch leading to a big, grassy backyard. The yard ran to a low cement wall placed at the sand line. Inserted into the wall were tall boards. Something she'd never seen before.

"We'll remove those, of course," said Bart, "now that summer's here. But they're handy protection for the house when winter winds blow the sand around."

"Makes sense," said Becca. "Not that I have any experience living at the beach."

"Then you're in for a treat this season. You'll come to love our peninsula with the ocean on one side and the bay on the other. There's always a breeze here. Know what I call this place?" His eyes gleamed, and he gestured widely to incorporate his world. "I call it our finger in the ocean."

He made life in Pilgrim Cove sound like a fairy tale, but Becca held back. Despite an easy ferry commute north to Boston, this paradise posed other challenges. Walking on soft sand was just the beginning. But…with the shady back porch, she could simply step outdoors and feast her eyes on the entire breathtaking scene. The ever-changing sky. The moody ocean. And the busy beach. No more living cooped up in a city apartment three stories above the street. The place she shared with Josie had no elevator, and remaining there was not an option. Compromise. Life was now about compromise.

"We'll have the porch furniture out here in a jiffy," said Bart as he unlocked the door. "And anything else that needs to be done."

Wide-planked oak floors ran throughout the house, chintz-covered couches and chairs, and in the kitchen, ample counter space. Three bedrooms. Three! Well, Josie and her boyfriend could visit—an easy enough trip from Boston. She hoped her mom would visit, too, maybe stay for a week or more, but she didn't count on it. Angela had missed work after the marathon. She lived in the western part of the state near the Berkshires and had stayed in Becca's apartment while Becca was in the hospital. She probably had no vacation days left and for sure would never sacrifice a day's pay.

Becca shrugged. She was on her own in Pilgrim Cove. *Deal with it.*

"We'll install the grab bars in the shower and anything else you think you'd need. Maybe a tall stool at the counter here? Easier to sit and stand again." Quinn paced the kitchen, looking for possibilities. "Would that suit?"

Suit? Becca's heartbeat quickened as she looked around. Outside, she'd have the sun, sea, porch, and a steady breeze. But inside this weathered ship, she'd be surrounded by sturdy walls, a cozy fireplace, and wide halls—with elbow room. No problem using a cane or wheelchair. Sea View House. An island of safety. And privacy. She'd get stronger here and return to normal. Oh, yeah. It would suit.

"How much, Mr. Quinn?"

He jumped back as if she'd slapped him. "How much, lassie? Why there's no charge for Sea View House. Not for you. This beauty is let on a sliding scale, part of the William Adams Foundation, who was shirttail cousin to John Adams, himself, and wasn't he the second president of the United States?"

The man spoke faster than she could hear, but she got the part about "no charge." She didn't buy it. Everything in life had a price. "Would you repeat that more slowly—about the rent?"

"No rent for you. The sliding scale, you see. By unanimous vote of the Board of Directors, of which I'm president."

Unbelievable. "Just to be clear, Mr. Quinn. Are you saying that this beautiful house—at least the first floor—is rent-free for the entire summer?"

"The first floor is called the Captain's Quarters, and that's exactly what I said, Ms. Rebecca. Rent-free. The question is, what do you say?"

"I say, where do I sign?"

Quinn laughed his big laugh. "Not to worry. I'll bring the papers around after you move in. I'll also bring the Sea View House journal, where you'll write your story."

Ahh. She knew there had to be a catch. "I'm no writer. Besides, the bombing's been in all the newspapers."

"Grammar doesn't count, girl! But stories do. It's a record, you see, about finding the magic again. You'll be able to catch up on all the folks who've stayed here before you. Like that professor you mentioned from Harvard who lived upstairs. Some other folks who've stayed here live in town now. In Pilgrim Cove. You'll probably meet them soon."

Not interested. Becca stared into the man's eyes, her gaze demanding his undivided attention. "Let's be perfectly clear, Mr. Quinn. My goal is to work hard and get strong enough to support myself later on—when I figure out how. I'll write something for you, but I'm not here to make friends or socialize. I had plenty of company in town after…after the explosions. Lots of attention and therapy. Sometimes too much. They were wonderful. Terrific people. But sometimes the hospital and the rehab center seemed like a madhouse to me. Now I need to be independent. On my own. Do you understand?" She wouldn't put it past him to send a few neighbors over just to stir things up.

"We'll do all we can to help you," said Bart. "Modifications and all. You'll be able to move in tomorrow."

Logistically perfect, but she sighed. He hadn't acknowledged a word about her wanting to be left alone.

#

Friday night and child-free. Adam Fielding, DVM, locked the door to his veterinary clinic, his newest retired greyhound at his side, and wondered what to do with his unexpected leisure time. Evening was a killer. The loneliest time of the day, the time when memories of Eileen were the strongest. Her laughter...that dimple tucked beside her sweet mouth... He'd loved pressing kisses against it. He missed cuddling on the couch, playing with her dark, curly hair, wrapping the strands around his fingers. Sara had inherited that feature. He missed Eileen's intelligence—her fast quips and thoughtful suggestions, a strong support for a debt-ridden young veterinarian just starting out. He yearned for his loving wife, his perfect wife. The perfect woman for him. He spoke to the grey.

"Neptune Park's probably opened for the season, but I'll save the carousel and Ferris wheel for Sara."

Ginger whined in agreement. Adam leaned over and scratched behind her small, folded-back ears. "Of course, Katie will come along." The intelligent dog, parti-colored with a white background and fawn patches, tilted her head, listening to Adam's every word. After a month with him and Sara, the dog had adapted well to being a house pet and was ready to adopt out. But Sara had other ideas for the pretty canine.

"No, Daddy. Not this one. She's special. I love her. Please..."

His daughter didn't have to beg. He'd give her the moon if she asked for it. As for the greyhounds...they were all special, at least to him. Each one faced a huge adjustment after living in a kennel since birth and after a life at the track. As he'd done with others, Adam had taken Ginger home from the rescue center in Boston, helped her to adjust to family living—house, car, kids, stairs, bed—until she'd be ready for a permanent family.

He shrugged. So now they'd have another personal pet. No problem. Dogs and cats got along, and the mighty Butterscotch ruled his roost with confidence. Sara's devotion to Ginger was odd, though. His daughter normally used her energy and wits finding good homes for abandoned pets. She knew they couldn't keep every rescue brought into the clinic. It seemed, however, Sara and Ginger had an understanding. They were a twosome. From his observation, Sara's love for the grey was being returned twice over.

Love. Easier between a dad and daughter or between a child and a puppy than between a man and a woman. He'd tried romance again after Eileen, a sensible relationship with Katie's mom. But they'd called off the engagement after Jason Parker returned to Pilgrim Cove. With one glance at Jason's love-stricken expression when he'd looked at Lila, Adam had recognized his own yearning for Eileen. He'd bowed out. Gracefully, too. And never looked back.

But their daughters remained inseparable—sisters of the heart. And now Jason and Lila were expecting a sibling for Katie. He wished them well. Sometimes, everything worked out, especially when no one harbored any grudges.

He meandered next door to the house he shared with his daughter and her changing menagerie. His stomach rumbled when he went inside, but he had no appetite for cooking or being alone. The Friday night Happy Hour and dinner at the Wayside Inn would suit. He'd probably run into a few friends or neighbors and have a congenial time. A perfect evening.

No more romantic involvements for him. He'd focus his energies on being the best dad a little girl could have. Between caring for Sara, running his animal hospital, and planning the addition of a greyhound rescue and fostering center, he'd hardly be lonely or bored.

The rescue expansion excited him. The start-up funding came from his own savings and a bit from the Boston Greyhound Foundation, where he volunteered his services. He was waiting for word about other funding, a big chunk, from a state-sponsored animal foundation. Life was good. Good enough, anyway.

After a quick shower, he slapped on some cologne, grabbed a clean jersey and jeans, and headed out.

#

Thirty minutes later, Adam stood at the bar, nursing a longneck with Rachel and Jack Levine. The couple had married recently and decided to live in Pilgrim Cove, Rachel's hometown.

"I didn't realize the Inn would be this crowded," said Rachel. "We were trying to avoid the hordes at the Lobster Pot tonight."

The Wayside Inn boasted a restaurant, bar, dance floor, spacious lobby, and guest rooms while somehow retaining the picturesque New England flavor at the same time.

"The summer season's the money season," Adam said.

"On a holiday weekend, every place is crowded," said Jack. "We should've stayed home."

"Well, I'm glad you didn't," said Adam. "My daughter's with Katie, so I'm on my own."

"Maybe not for long." Rachel grinned and inclined her head toward two attractive brunettes several seats down the bar. "New in town. No gold bands. Let's welcome them to Pilgrim Cove." She shifted from her stool, starting to match action to her words.

"Whoa, Nelly! You're not the welcoming committee." Jack wrapped his arm around his wife, stopping her descent, and Adam breathed a sigh of relief. The man had his back, whether he realized it or not. Adam had no desire for small talk with strangers.

"Why not?" protested Rachel. "We're in Pilgrim Cove, not Manhattan. It's the start of summer, and everyone's on vacation and in a good mood. In another month, I will be, too."

"Some of us," drawled Jack, "work twelve months a year. Like Adam and me."

While the couple bantered, Adam glanced at the two women, who were now following a hostess toward a table. His brow narrowed. Something was off, and he continued to track their progress.

"The prettier one's got trouble. Big trouble," he muttered just as the woman turned toward him, head on an angle. She met his gaze, and her chin rose. Her brown eyes turned the shade of bitter cocoa, and as swiftly as she'd engaged him, she showed him her back.

Adam burned. Whether from embarrassment or anger, he couldn't discern. He couldn't think! The woman's eyes were as dark as Eileen's, her hair as chestnut brown and wavy as Sara's.... He needed air.

#

"The last thing I expect or need is to be hit on. Did you see that guy?" Becca leaned across the table toward her cousin. "But I think I scared him off."

"Sure, I saw him," said Josie. "Hard to miss Tall, Hazel, and Handsome. Easy on the eyes. But he was all about you, cuz. That is so cool!"

Meeting a nice guy in a bar might have been cool in the old days—not that this guy seemed "nice" at all. He'd studied her like a specimen on a Petri dish, and she wouldn't put up with that. If she ran into him again, she'd say so. But more important was the big picture. Today began her new tomorrow. The old days were gone.

"I don't need anyone in my life, Josie. I'm not in the market for pity or being second best. I'd rather be alone."

"Oh, please." Josie waved away her protestations as if slapping a gnat.

"You're only second best in your own mind. That guy was looking and looking hard."

"Until he saw me walk."

"You're imagining things."

But she hadn't imagined that. He'd stared at her so hard she'd felt the burn. And then she'd met his gaze and given as good as she'd gotten. She'd be willing to bet her bottom dollar—which was about all she had—that the only looks she'd receive from now on were those of curiosity and pity. Her hands clenched into fists. Not for her! She'd deal with those men like she'd dealt with Tall, Hazel, and Handsome tonight. Just return their stares with one of her own.

#

As though Bart Quinn really was King of the Elves, the necessary modifications to her apartment started the very next day. Bart himself was overseeing the changes, the two children at his side. Furniture was moved, nonslip mats were placed under rugs, and grab bars were installed in the walk-in shower along with a plastic chair. Grab bars went on the wall by the tub, too.

These conveniences were essential. She had jotted notes to herself about the adjustments she'd need, but she wondered aloud how Bart Quinn had figured them out.

"Papa Bart knows everything," said Katie with a hard shake of her head and satisfaction in her voice. "That's what Grandma always says."

Bart's laughter had Becca joining in. "Not quite, lassie. But I like your version better. My daughters would say I just *think* I know everything."

"There's a difference," said Becca, smiling as she glanced from Katie to her loyal shadow. Sara leaned against "Papa Bart" as though she belonged to him, also. Sensitive. Lonely. Something was going on inside the sweet girl. Becca looked away. Not her business.

"Bart's friends are amazing, too," Josie said as they watched the house fix-it operation progress. "All sharper than their age."

"I agree," said Becca. "The shoemaker had his elves, but we have the ROMEOs. And the name fits them. These Retired Old Men Eating Out have the energy of guys ten years their junior. You'd think they owned the town the way they talk about it."

Rick O'Brien, retired police chief, had come to assure her that Sea View House had withstood many a hurricane and not to worry. He provided several flashlights and a supply of batteries. The electrician, Ralph Bigelow, had already guaranteed that her air conditioning wouldn't let her down. She'd thanked him but really wanted a sea breeze! And then came Doc

Rosen. Retired or not, the man had eyes that missed nothing. He could be an incredible ally.

"I know everyone at our community hospital," he'd said, "including the physical therapists in Outpatient. You call me with any question that comes up."

"Thanks," she said. "I hope to lead a very quiet life here. No emergencies, please. And I'll be taking most of my P.T. in Boston at the rehab center. I'm using the ferry service." She grinned. "Who knew people commuted by ferry? It'll be fun." If she didn't lose her balance when the boat rocked.

"Excellent! But my offer stands. If you need support in any way, you call us. My wife...my wife is a breast cancer survivor. We know about long-term treatment, timely treatment. We know personally how important it is to have people in your corner."

She struggled to find words. She'd never known men like these. They didn't know her but for two days, so why would they care so much? Her own dad...she'd barely known him. He'd died much too young, when she was only five years old. So what did she really know about dads and granddads? Not much.

Time to discover if these guys meant what they said. She walked through the center hall toward the bedrooms. "My first decision is about exercising. Dr. Rosen, which room would you choose as the best place for doing home therapy?"

"How wide is your mat and how wide are these beds?" asked the doctor. "The mat needs to be centered, not sticking out over the sides." He peered into the first guest room.

"More company's coming!" Josie's voice rang through the house, a voice tinged with excitement.

"Knock, knock." Another voice. This time mellow, deep, and definitely male.

EXCERPT FROM
THE HOUSE ON THE BEACH
(PILGRIM COVE SERIES BOOK ONE)

"I'm sorry, Ali, but I'm not ready to make such a big decision." Laura McCloud sat at the kitchen table across from her sister the morning after their mother's funeral sipping coffee and nibbling a piece of dry toast. Her Boston home had overflowed with visitors the evening before, but she and Ali were alone now. The house was almost back in order. Leftovers filled the refrigerator shelves—not that she had much of an appetite.

"But you know how much we'd love for you to join us in Atlanta," continued Alison. "Charles especially wants you to know that the invitation comes from him, too. And the kids would adore having their Aunt Laura close by."

"I do know it, and I love you all for it, but...

"And we have fabulous medical centers, too," interrupted Alison. "As good as here. Not that you have anything to worry about anymore," she added quickly.

Right. Nothing except the knowledge that there were no guarantees. "I'm not concerned about finding medical care. It's just that I have another idea."

"You do? What?"

"Remember Pilgrim Cove? Remember the beautiful beach?" Laura watched her sister's eyes widen and a grin light up her face.

"Do I remember? Of course I remember. What great summers we had. So, what's your idea? A summer vacation at the beach?"

"Not exactly," replied Laura. "I'm not going to wait that long."

"You're going to the beach in the middle of winter?" Alison asked in disbelief as she hugged herself. "Brr. Not me."

Laura laughed at her sister's antics. They'd always gotten along well, and Laura had really missed Alison when she'd left Boston. Suddenly, Laura had to blink back tears. Alison was now her only family.

"I'll think about what you said regarding Atlanta, but I've got a career here and...I need some time. Time for myself."

Alison's hand reached for hers. "I'll support any decision you make, sis, but are you sure you really want to be alone?"

"With the sand and the ocean and my work...don't worry, Ali. I'll be very busy."

"Yeah, yeah. The sand will blow in your eyes, the ocean will crash against the seawall and the ferry won't run. So much for winter at the beach!"

Laura smiled. "I'll wait until next month. March should be somewhat better. I wonder what Pilgrim Cove is like during the off-season. At least the rent should be cheaper."

"Wait a minute. Why are you concerned about rent? A few dollars one way or another for a week's vacation shouldn't make a difference."

"I'm thinking about more than a week," Laura said in a slow, deliberate tone. "I'm thinking about a three month lease, maybe through Memorial Day. A small house might not be too expensive, not too hard to keep up, but I'd want it right on the beach."

She stood as the image crystallized in her mind. "I need a change, a complete change of scene. And I need it now. Fighting with the weather will be much easier than fighting for mom's life and my own." She reached up and tousled her short blonde curls. "Look at me, Alison. Look at these ringlets. I'm delighted to have hair again, but I don't recognize myself when I pass a mirror. Where's the sleek blunt cut that was so easy to manage?"

"You're adorable in those curls! In fact, you look wonderful, Laura, just wonderful." Laura could hear the passion in her sister's voice.

"Donald didn't think so," she responded.

"Donald Crawford was a jerk!"

Laura shook her head. "No, Alison. Don wasn't a jerk. He was just human. He had a girlfriend with a huge responsibility to an ill mother—and he handled that—but my getting sick was just too much. He wasn't prepared for all the emotional turmoil. Who can blame him?"

"I can," replied Alison.

"Be fair," said Laura. "We weren't engaged. He didn't owe me anything."

"He wasn't worthy of you!" Alison insisted. "You're the most outstanding person, the most beautiful, wonderful woman...

"You're hardly objective," laughed Laura. "But can you really blame Don for wanting a normal life? What man wouldn't have second thoughts when he heard the words 'breast cancer?'"

"A man who loves you," came the quick reply.

"Well, I'm not going to count on that happening," said Laura in an even tone. "So I'll have lots of time and energy to rebuild my interrupted career." She leaned across the table. "I'm thirty-three. It's now or never. And you heard my agent last night. 'Work is therapy, Laura,' she mimicked Norman Cohen's low voice. She relaxed in her chair. "Norman is a dear friend as well as a business man. And he's got some radio ads lined up for me."

Alison would have protested again, but Laura held up her hand. "I'm not discussing men anymore, Ali. I'm not sure there's a man in the world who could look past this. Anyway, it's too soon. All I can do is take one day at a time. *Capice?*"

"Sure," replied Alison. "I understand, but I don't have to like it. I love you, and I want you to have..."

"I know," Laura said in a hoarse voice. "You want me to have everything you have...loving husband, healthy children...but that's probably not going to happen for me. What is going to happen, however, is a nice long stay in Pilgrim Cove."

Alison remained quiet for a long moment. "I recognize that expression and that tone," she finally said. "You've made up your mind. But my invitation remains open—will always remain open."

Laura looked at her sister's face, at the sincerity clearly written there. "Thanks, Ali, thanks a lot. But I've got to figure it out my own way."

She reached for the phone. "I'm calling Bartholomew Quinn, the man who arranged the summer rentals when we were kids. I remember going with

Daddy to Mr. Quinn's real estate office. And I remember him. A head of thick white hair."

"White? And that was how many years ago? Sixteen? Seventeen? He might be dead by now!"

"Nope. He had a website."

#

Bartholomew Quinn stood at the large front window of his Main Street office in Pilgrim Cove, his hand cupping the bowl of the empty pipe in his mouth. A comfortable habit he hadn't bothered to break even though he'd given up the pleasure of filling the beauty with fine tobacco.

Promises. He'd made promises. A promise to his daughters and to his beloved granddaughter and to her precious daughter. Four generations of Quinns, three of whom had said, "No more smoking, Dad, Granddad, Papa Bart!" He shook his head remembering how they'd ganged up on him. Foolish girls to worry so much. He was as strong as ever and as sharp as ever, and maybe just as hard-headed, too. He sighed. Except these days he chomped an empty pipe.

His eyes focused on the late model blue Honda Accord pulling into a visitor's spot in front of his building, then he glanced at his watch. If this was Laura McCloud, she was right on time. He'd been astonished to hear from her last week. Astonished that she remembered him. But then again, he grinned to himself, he was a pretty memorable guy. Just ask his kids. Or anyone in Pilgrim Cove. Everyone knew Bartholomew Quinn!

The car door opened and a woman emerged, golden hair tossing in the wind. Bart tsked. She should have worn a hat. Wasn't she aware that February was the worst of the winter months in New England? He straightened his silk bow tie and adjusted the comfortable woolen cardigan he wore. Bart Quinn knew how to adapt to weather and to life. After seventy-five years on the planet, he'd had plenty of practice.

He watched the young woman check the sign—Quinn Real Estate and Property Management—and walk to the front door. He went to greet her.

"Well, as I live and breathe," he said, shaking Laura's hand. "The young McCloud girl. All grown up."

She had a delightful laugh, but it didn't quite hide the sadness in her dark blue eyes. Strain showed in the too-thin face.

"Come in and have a hot cup of Earl Grey." He ushered her to a small round table. After calling to an assistant for the tea, he took a seat opposite Laura.

"You've had a hard time of it, haven't you?" Bart began. "A fine woman was Bridget McCloud, and your dad, too. I remember Connor well. Two good people, and now their daughter's come to see me." He sat back in his chair and waited.

Laura nodded. "Yes, I've come to you, Mr. Quinn, with a request." She moved her chair a fraction closer. "My question is, can you help me find a house to rent immediately? A house right on the beach. I want to be able to open my eyes and see the ocean."

Her voice had the clarity of a bell. A musical quality, Bart thought. She was so lovely despite her distress. He cocked his head as he listened.

"I-I need to get away for awhile," Laura continued. "I need to be here, near the water. Can't wait for summer. I need to...to..."

"Lick your wounds? Heal a little?" suggested Bart.

Her eyes widened. "That's part of it. Mom's illness...she was in remission for so long, and then three years ago, the nightmare began again. Her nerve cells deteriorated. In the end, she couldn't walk, couldn't talk... I need some time to recover and to adjust." She paused in thought. "Long walks on the beach, fresh air, time to read, and to cook simple meals. And with some basic recording equipment, I can work here as well as in Boston."

"And what exactly does Laura McCloud do to earn her keep?"

A dimple appeared as she shot him a small grin. "Laura McCloud earns her keep on the radio and telly with her commercial announcements."

Her language and Irish lilt matched his, and he roared with laughter. "Oh, you've got it down, girl." Bart was pure American, but his parents had emigrated from County Cork at the turn of the last century and a bit of their flavorful speech had taken hold in him.

She nodded. "I've always been good at languages. I seem to have the ear and the voice. In college, I majored in Speech and Theater and found my work in narration and voice-overs. But," she turned away from him then and stared through the window, "my career has fallen apart in the last few years. I've been...distracted. And now I've got to rebuild."

Her eyes glowed as she turned to him again, and Bart saw the strength behind them. This girl would make it somehow, with or without his help. But he wanted very much to help her. He thought about a property he managed—a unique beach front property—with a sliding scale rental fee for people in difficult circumstances. His gut told him Laura qualified, and his gut was rarely wrong. He nodded his head. "Sea View House."

"Excuse me?"

"You'll be wanting Sea View House." Bart stood up and walked to his big old-fashioned roll-top desk, selected a key from among many on his ring, and opened a small drawer. He reached for one set of duplicate keys and relocked the drawer. Picking up the phone, he pressed the intercom. "Lila, come in and meet a special friend of mine." He winked at Laura and opened his office door just as Lila rushed through.

Bart chuckled. Lila never walked.

"Laura McCloud," he said, "I'd like you to meet my partner, Lila Quinn Sullivan, who also happens to be my granddaughter.

#

Bart's granddaughter was lovely, thought Laura, as she extended her hand. Twenty-something. Bright blue eyes, with an intelligence behind them.

"I'm looking for a place to rent," Laura said. "Your grandfather suggested Sea View House."

The girl looked startled before a wistful expression replaced her surprise. "Sea View House." Her soft-spoken words were followed by a sweet smile. "It's a special place."

"Yes," Bart confirmed. "And Laura's a special guest. Used to spend summers here as a child." He looked at Laura. "About ten consecutive years, was it?"

She nodded. "What's so special about this particular house on the beach?" She needed a quiet routine, nothing out of the ordinary.

Lila stared over Laura's shoulder, her eyes unfocused and dreamy. "Sea View House has this reputation," she began. "Good things happen to everyone who stays there...." She paused, then shook her head, a flash of pain visible for barely a second. "Well, no. I guess not everyone...but, I know *you'll* be happy there, with the ocean right at your door. Welcome back to Pilgrim Cove."

And she was gone.

"Moves at the speed of light, my Lila does," said Bart, as he led Laura to his car. "She's the joy of my life, she and her little Katie. But...well, there's a sorrow on her heart, too." He sighed. "Everybody's got troubles, but I can't think of a better place to be than Sea View House while you figure them out."

Laura murmured noncommittally. She scanned the town as they drove, excitement mounting as she recognized some of the businesses. From Bart's office on Main Street, they passed a bank, then a barber shop called The Cove Clippers. She'd gone there with her dad each year for his "summer cut." And there was The Diner on the Dunes! Happy times and delicious meals with her family.

"There's Parker Plumbing and Hardware," Bart pointed out. "They carry everything. I'll call Matt to turn your water on. My friend, Sam Parker, started the business, but now his son, Matthew, runs it. Good family. Not without their share of heartaches, too. But they carry on."

Laura sighed. If Bart thought he was giving her a lesson in life, he was wasting his time. She was already an expert. But she didn't interrupt him, instead continued to look at the town, trying to recognize landmarks from her childhood.

"Is Neptune's Park still here?" she asked.

Bart grinned around his pipe. "Sure it is. Can't imagine Pilgrim Cove without it, but it's only open in the summertime, mind you."

She nodded. Carousels and Ferris wheels were the stuff of sunshine and warm nights. Too bad she wouldn't be in town long enough to enjoy them. She refocused on the route Bart was taking and memorized it. He made a left from Main onto Outlook Drive.

"The whole peninsula is six miles long and less than two miles across, so we'll be at Sea View House in just a couple of minutes. Main Street divides the town. We have a beach side and a bay side. There's always a breeze when you're a finger in the ocean."

"That's why you have so many summer people every year," Laura said. "The news is out. Pilgrim Cove is the place to be during the season."

"For me, it's the place to be every season," said Bart. "Look ahead now. You'll see the front and side of the house.

Laura complied and felt herself grinning. Sea View House. Weathered wood, a big sloping roof, two stories with a third window above—maybe an attic—and a big brick chimney in the center. A white picket fence surrounded the front yard on Beach Street.

"Wow! What a wonderful house. And only a vague memory to me. I didn't know anyone living here when I was a kid."

Bart pulled the car into the driveway. "It's a Saltbox, the kind built in the 1700's. John Adams, our second president, was born in a Saltbox. And William Adams, a shirt-tail cousin of John, founded our town in 1690. A hundred years later his great-great grandchild, also named William, built this house. Of course, it's been remodeled several times, and now it's been converted to two apartments. There's a lot of history here, but for a later time."

Laura nodded and got out of the car. "Let's walk around the house first," she said.

"You go. I'll open her up," replied Bart. "The sun is bright enough, but that ocean breeze is whipping big today."

True, but Laura reveled in it as she followed the paved driveway to the back of the property, past a deep covered porch leading to a backyard bordered by a low cement wall at the sand line. Inserted into the cement wall were tall boards standing upright. Laura studied the strange arrangement and saw loose sand blowing against the boards. Sand that would otherwise be hitting the house. She smiled, appreciating the simplicity of some solutions.

And then she was on the beach, the powerful Atlantic in front of her, surging and ebbing as far as her eye could see. The heels of her boots hardly dented the hard packed sand as she walked closer to the water. She could have stood for hours mesmerized by the rhythmic motion of the waves. She turned, eventually, to look back at Sea View House.

For the first time in too long, a frisson of excitement flowed through her. A sense of anticipation. Suddenly she knew exactly what she was going to do.

She hurried to the front door, ran down the center hallway and found Bart Quinn in the kitchen. "Where do I sign?"

LINDA BARRETT BOOKS

NOVELS—ROMANCE

No Ordinary Family Series
Unforgettable (Bk. 1)

Safe at Home (Bk. 2)

Heartstrings (Bk. 3)

His Greatest Catch (Bk. 4)

The Broken Circle (Bk. 5)

Starting Over Series

True-Blue Texan (Bk 1)

A Man of Honor (Bk. 2)

Love, Money and Amanda Shaw (Bk.3)

The Inn at Oak Creek (Bk.4)

Flying Solo Series

Summer at the Lake (Bk. 1)

Houseful of Strangers (Bk. 2)

Quarterback Daddy (Bk. 3)

The Apple Orchard (Bk. 4)

Pilgrim Cove Series

The House on the Beach (Bk. 1)

No Ordinary Summer (Bk. 2)

Reluctant Housemates (Bk. 3)

The Daughter He Never Knew (Bk. 4)

Sea View House Series

Her Long Walk Home (Bk. 1)

Her Picture-Perfect Family (Bk. 2)

Her Second-Chance Hero (Bk. 3)

NOVELS—WOMEN'S FICTION

The Broken Circle

The Soldier and the Rose

Family Interrupted

For Better or Worse – A boxed set of all three WF novels at a discounted price

SHORT NOVELLA

Man of the House

MEMOIR

HOPEFULLY EVER AFTER: Breast Cancer, Life and Me (true story about surviving breast cancer twice)